Burned Out

Firehouse Blues Series: Book 3

AE Moran

Invisible Publishing Company

Firehouse Blues Series

Contents

Chapter 1: Emily

"There's our new house!" I pull the rental car up to the curb and gaze at my new house through the windshield.

My seven-year-old son Zeke unclips his seatbelt and climbs onto the passenger seat so he can see. "Mom—it's beautiful!" he gasps.

"Yeah, it is!" I sigh and feast my eyes on the sight beyond the sidewalk.

The sweet little cottage sits back from the street surrounded by a four-foot brick wall. Roses climb all over the wall, up the side posts, and over the front porch.

Flowers and ornamental trees cluster in the front yard. The house looks like something out of a fairy tale—my fairy tale.

Zeke pushes open the passenger door. "Come on, Mom! Let's go check it out! I want to see everything!"

He takes off running and leaves the car door flapping in the breeze. I only smile at him. We've both waited so long for this. This house is going to be a dream come true for both of us.

I take longer to park, shut his door, and then open the hatchback. I take out our suitcases and wheel them to the wooden gate leading through the garden wall.

Everything about this place reminds me of a storybook setting where any magical thing might happen. The brick-walled front yard, porch, and the front door look even better in real life than they did in the pictures.

I wheel the suitcases into the front hall and stop there to take in the scene. Stairs rise to the second story. A polished wooden banister runs up next to the stairs and plush brown velvet carpet covers the steps.

Hardwood floors lead down the front entrance hall to the kitchen. The living room and another sitting room occupy each side of the hall. Both rooms have bay windows looking out into the front garden.

Zeke comes charging into the house through the back door at the end of the hall. "This house is awesome, Mom!" he yells. "This place has everything!"

I laugh at him. "Go upstairs and pick out which room you want. Once you do that, come help me unload the car." He takes off upstairs and I yell after him, "I'm not doing all the work by myself!"

He pretends to ignore me and vanishes down the landing at the top of the stairs. I assume the bedrooms are there. That will make him and them easy to find.

I go back out to the car and bring in a bunch of boxes. I check the labels on the outside and take three of them to the kitchen.

It's an old farmhouse-style kitchen with a big wooden table and an iron rack hanging over the stove. This is perfect. Everything about this house is perfect.

I open one of the boxes, take out my potted plants, and set them on the windowsill above the sink. Another window looks out into the backyard.

It's much bigger than it looked in the pictures. More flowering trees and flowerbeds surround a grassy lawn leading down to some fruit trees at the very bottom. A wooden fence encloses everything and ivy grows on the fence to make the whole yard feel private and comfortable.

I smile through the window. I'm really going to love living here. I can already feel it.

I turn back to the job at hand and take out a handful of kitchen utensils from the bottom of the box. I get a rush of satisfaction when I hang them on the rack above the stove. They look nice up there and give the kitchen a homey, lived-in feel.

I put the empty box on the floor, but I'm not supposed to start unpacking boxes until I unload the car.

I go back out there. Boxes, bedding, and overstuffed bags fill every inch of space in the entire car except for the two front seats. I even jammed a few loaded bags into the hollow in front of the front passenger seat where Zeke's feet are supposed to go.

I spend another hour carrying boxes into the living room and kitchen before I realize that I haven't seen Zeke in a while. He isn't helping, the little rat. Where could he be?

The upstairs bedrooms are supposed to be empty except for the basic furniture. He couldn't have found anything interesting to do up there. Then again, that kid can find something interesting to do just about anywhere.

I finish taking stuff to the living room and kitchen. Then I take Zeke's suitcase and bedding upstairs. I leave everything on the landing while I try to decide which room he's picked out for himself.

It isn't immediately obvious because he isn't up here. I go from room to room calling, "Zeke! Buddy! Sweetheart! Where are you?"

I stick my head into each room. Then I come to the master bedroom at the end of the hall. An old-fashioned four-poster bed occupies the center. The carpet looks a little threadbare, but I can live with that. I'll just cover it up with another throw rug.

Another bay window looks out over the backyard and I stop there to gaze out at it. The trees, flowers, and greenery relax my mind. I could stand at this window forever and never get tired of looking out there.

That settles it. This is going to be my room. I love it already. I can't wait to move in. I get a thrill when I remember that I'm going to sleep in here tonight—and every night after this.

I turn away feeling a fresh surge of energy to unload the car and unpack everything—especially my own things. I really want to move into this room and start living here.

I get back out to the landing where I get confronted again by Zeke's luggage. I guess he's leaving it up to me to decide which room is his since he didn't tell me.

The other three bedrooms are much smaller and not as nice, but still comfortable. One has a queen bed in it. The second one has two single beds and the third, smallest bedroom has one single bed.

I choose the last one and park Zeke's stuff at the end of the bed. He can unpack his own stuff since he thinks it's okay to run off and leave me to do everything else.

I go to the car and throw caution to the wind by taking my own things up to the master bedroom. I feel an overwhelming flood of happiness when I hang my clothes in the closet and put my keepsakes on the dusty old wooden dresser across the room.

This is my room. It's all mine. I don't have to share it with any-one—except for Zeke if he wants to come and cuddle up with me in here.

I sigh as I put the last of my shirts and underwear in the dresser drawers and my shoes on the closet floor. Now I'm all ready to spend tonight in here. This room is mine and it's all ready and waiting for me when I come back.

I go back downstairs. That's when I notice the silence. I don't hear Zeke anywhere.

I stick my head out the back door and yell, "Zeke! Where are you?"

Nothing. He doesn't answer. I stand there and listen. I don't hear him moving around anywhere. That's strange. He usually makes a lot of noise no matter what he's doing.

He definitely isn't in the backyard.

I go back inside and yell up the stairs even though I was just up there. I would have heard if he was up there in any of the bedrooms.

"Zeke!" I yell. "Where are you, sweetie?"

I don't hear anything and I get a very bad feeling about this. I stride out to the car, but of course he isn't in it anymore. "Zeke!" I yell through the front yard. "Zeke! Answer me!"

He doesn't answer and the silence keeps getting more oppressive.

I race back inside and go room to room calling for him. "Zeke! Zeke! Where are you?"

He doesn't answer and I keep not finding him. I stop in the middle of the living room with my heart hammering out of my chest. He can't be gone—not when I just went to all the trouble of getting my dream house. This was supposed to be the place where he and I would finally be happy.

I can't stand here thinking he's gone. I scramble to pull my phone out of my pocket. My hands shake as I dial 911.

"911 emergency dispatch," a raspy older woman's voice answers on the other end of the line. "Please state the nature of the emergency."

"My son....." I gasp. "My son....he just disappeared....out of the house.....He was here....and now he's gone! I've searched everywhere! He isn't here!"

"How long has he been gone, Ma'am?" the woman asked.

"Uh.....I don't know.....maybe....." I try to think. How long *has* Zeke been gone? I've lost track of time. I can't be sure. "Maybe half an hour......I don't know....."

"I'm dispatching Police and Fire Department crews to your location now, Ma'am," she replies and then repeats back the address. "Please stay on the line until they arrive."

"Uh.....okay....." I choke.

I can't stop trembling and my skin goes cold while I pace around the house pressing the phone to my ear. He can't be gone. He can't be. He's all I have.

I go from room to room while I wait just to be sure. That would be just like Zeke to turn up in one of the rooms after I already panicked and called the Police to find him.

He isn't here. I check the backyard again, but he isn't there, either. The fence encloses the yard on all sides.

I find a gate in the fence at the very bottom of the backyard. It leads to the house next door. I climb onto the fence rail and look over, but Zeke isn't there, either.

I go back inside just as a huge fire truck pulls up to the curb. It parks behind my rental car and a bunch of firefighters get out. They're all wearing their heavy protective overalls and jackets, but not their helmets—of course. There's no fire.

Two Police squad cars pull up right behind the fire truck and then a bright red pickup with Fire Department branding emblazoned on the side shows up.

A tall, broad-shouldered man with black hair gets out of the pickup. He wears blue pants, heavy black leather boots, and a blue Fire Department uniform T-shirt.

He exchanges a few words with the firefighters and they all laugh. Then he meets up with the Police officers. I hang up the phone as they all enter the front yard and I go out onto the porch to meet them.

Chapter 2: Danny

I kick back on the couch, prop my tennis shoes on the arm, and stretch out with my head on the cushion. Now I'm fully relaxed with a glass of cold lemonade at my elbow. I can finally face the ordeal in front of me.

I pick up the folder of Professional Development paperwork and open it. I start reading the welcome letter that explains all the hoops I have to jump through to get my next Professional Development certification. I can't wait.

Just then, movement catches my eye coming from the kitchen. I don't have any trouble putting the paperwork down to see what it is even though it probably isn't anything important.

I look up to see a little boy standing on my back porch. He holds his hands around his eyes so he can peer through the sliding glass door into my house. The little rascal. What is he doing here?

I sit up and his eyes fall out of their sockets when he sees me get to my feet. That's right, you little scamp. You better be scared.

He stands there gaping at me in horror as I cross the dining room to the glass door. I slide it back and tower over him. He can't be more than seven and he's shaking like a leaf.

"I'm....sorry....Mister....." he stammers. "I didn't know there was anyone home."

"What are you doing here, kid?" I glance behind me. "How did you get back here? I didn't hear you go through the side gate."

"I didn't go through the side gate. I came through that gate over there."

He points to the gate in the fence at the bottom of my backyard. It connects to the house next door. No one has used that gate in years—definitely not since I've lived here.

I frown at the gate and then at the house next door. "How did you get over there? No one lives over there."

"They do now," he tells me. "Me and my mom just moved in."

My eyebrows fly up. "You did? Since when?"

"Since this morning. We just pulled in."

"Is that so?"

He nods fast. "Yeah."

"Well, then, welcome to the neighborhood." I stick out my hand. "I'm Danny. What's your name?"

He stares at me in shock for a second and then glances down at my hand. He has to think about it before he decides to shake my hand. "I'm Zeke—Zeke Montgomery."

"It's good to meet you, Zeke. It looks like we're gonna be next-door neighbors."

"Yeah." He squirms and his eyes dart past me into the house.

I'm not doing anything other than reading up on my Professional Development. God knows I'll take any excuse to get out of that, so I wave behind me. "Do you want to come in?"

I slide the door back and stand aside. He steps across the threshold and immediately starts looking around like that's what he came here to do in the first place. If I wasn't home, he probably would have come inside and explored the place anyway.

I go back to the couch and sit down, but I put my paperwork aside. I'll do that later.....sometime.

He finally makes his way into the living room. "Do you live here by yourself?" he asks.

"Yep. It's just me. What about you? Do you have any brothers or sisters—or is it just you and your mom?"

"Just me and my mom. We like it that way."

I nod. "Good plan."

He frowns at me. "So.....you don't have any kids?"

I feel my face flush. "No, I don't have any kids—not yet. Maybe someday I will."

His face falls. "Oh. I was hoping there would be some kids next door that I could play with."

"I know plenty of kids. I could introduce you."

His eyes light up. "You do? You could?"

"Sure. I know tons of kids....and they all go to the school down the block over there. You'll probably get to know them when you start going to school there."

His expression bursts into a huge, beaming grin. "That would be great!"

"Cool. That solves that problem, then."

He smiles at the house again and then frowns at me. "What's that?"

I look down to see what he's pointing at. He's pointing at my shirt. "That's the Fire Department logo. I'm a firefighter. The firehouse is right down the block from the school over there. That's where I work."

His eyes fly open all over again. "You're a firefighter?! For real?!"

"Yeah." I find myself blushing again. "It's great."

"That would be awesome! So do you get to go up the ladder and go into burning buildings and all that kind of stuff? For real?"

"Yeah. That's my job. I just went into a burning building yesterday, actually. I got an old lady and her granddaughter out—me and the other firefighters, that is. I didn't do it alone."

"That is so cool!" he gushes. "I wish I could be a firefighter."

"Maybe you could. See? Look at this.'"

I lead him over to the mantel shelf over the fireplace and take down a picture of me and my brother John shaking hands with the mayor and the Chief of Police. The oak-framed case includes a side panel with a gold cross attached by a ribbon.

"This is my Medal of Valor and this is a picture of me receiving it from the mayor and the Chief of Police."

"Who's that?" Zeke points to John.

"That's my brother, John. He's the fire chief. He runs the firehouse. He's actually my boss." I take down another case with five other decorations. "This one is the Commendation for Heroism. I got it when I went into a building to save three kids who were trapped. The building collapsed while we were all inside and the building collapsed on top of me."

He gasps and looks up at me with huge eyes. "No way! You didn't die?"

I laugh at him. "Of course not. I'm still alive, aren't I? I threw myself over the kids and made a little tent for them with my body. I got four broken ribs and I stayed like that for ten hours before anyone found us. The fire crew had to put out the fire first and then they went through the wreckage and found me and the kids. I spent two months in the hospital for that one."

"Whoa!" he breathes. "That is so awesome."

I put the case back on the mantel. "Anyway, I could tell you a million stories. Every day is another story. That's what's so cool about it."

I go back to the couch and sit down. Zeke follows me and stands in front of me where he was before. This is so much more interesting than reading my Professional Development booklet.

"My mom will never let me be a firefighter," he murmurs.

"Why not? I'm sure she'd be very proud if you did. My mom has three sons who are all firefighters and I know she's proud of all of us."

"You're lucky," he grumbles. "My mom freaks out every time anything happens even if it isn't dangerous. She freaks out over the tiniest little thing. She never lets me do anything."

I have to chuckle. "That's because she loves you and she doesn't want you to get hurt. Besides, you're just a kid now. You'll grow up and she won't be so protective. My mom was the same way when we were little."

"Really?" he asks.

I shrug. "Well, she had three boys, so she kinda had to let us do dangerous things. It's probably different because you're all your mom has. Of course she wants to protect you, but when you get older, she'll realize that you have to go out there and push yourself. That's the way it is when you're young."

He sighs. "I wish I was big now."

"I get it, buddy. I used to feel that way, too. I used to wish I was as big and as strong as my brothers so I could beat them up instead of the other way around. Then I grew up." I laugh at the memory.

"So did you beat them up?" he asks.

I burst out laughing. "No, I didn't beat them up. We all became firefighters and now we all work on the same team. I respect them too much as men to beat them up—even if they make me mad sometimes."

"You're lucky," he tells me. "I hate being a kid."

"It gets better when you get older. I promise." I can't stop myself from rumpling his hair. "Are you hungry or thirsty? Do you want some lemonade or a sandwich?"

"Okay. Thanks."

He follows me into the kitchen and climbs onto one of the bar stools while I tear into the fridge. I pour him a glass of lemonade and then start making sandwiches for both of us.

He watches me while he sips his lemonade. "How come you don't have any kids?" he blurts out.

I shrug and concentrate on my sandwiches so I don't have to make eye contact with him. "I don't know. I guess it just hasn't worked out that way yet. It will happen someday, though. I'm not that old."

"How old are you?" he asks.

I grin at him. I love how frank and unfiltered he is. It really is refreshing just to have a normal conversation with him. "I'm twenty-six."

"Wow, you're really old!" he exclaims.

I bite back laughter and hand him a sandwich. "Thanks a lot, pal. How old are you?"

"Seven...but I'll be eight in two months."

"Well, then you'll be really old, too. You might find this hard to believe, but you'll be twenty-six pretty soon, too."

"Naw," he tells me. "I'll never be that old."

I sit down on the next bar stool and we both start eating. He takes a huge bite and starts chewing, but after only a few seconds, he stops and his eyes dart around the kitchen while he holds the bulge of food in his cheek.

"What's wrong?" I ask him. "Is it no good?"

He gulps and tries to chew at the same time. "Um....what time is it?"

"I don't know." I glance at my watch. "It's eleven-thirty. Why?"

"My mom might not want me to eat lunch this early. I should have asked her first."

Now it's my turn to freeze with a mouthful of sandwich stuffed into my cheek. "You.....you didn't tell your mom where you were going?"

He shakes his head. "I should have told her that, too."

I start chewing again, but I've suddenly lost my appetite for anything to eat. "Finish your sandwich and then I'll take you home and explain it to her. I don't want her to worry about where you are."

Chapter 3: Emily

I dash down the porch steps and meet up with the Police and firemen in the front yard. "Thank God you're here! I searched the whole house more than once. We just moved in, so he doesn't know his way around."

"We'll find him, Ma'am. Don't worry," the tall, dark-haired Fire Department guy tells me and holds out his hand. "I'm Fire Chief John Brewer. This is my brother Kieth and this is Billy Cates."

He indicates two huge, burly, gorilla-type firemen with him. Chief Brewer's brother has a rough brown beard and looks like a biker. A wicked scar cuts across his forehead and disappears in his hair.

"How old is your son?" Chief Brewer asks me.

"He's only seven and he explores everything. I thought he was in the backyard, but I already checked at least ten times."

He turns to the men with him. "Spread out and establish a perimeter around the house. After that, we'll do a systematic concentric search of the neighborhood." He turns to the two Police officers. "If you two could establish checkpoints around the neighborhood and then alert the neighbors, I'd appreciate it."

"You got it, Chief," one of them replies and the two officers leave.

Chief Brewer turns back to me. "If you don't mind, I'd like my guys to go into your house and search it. I know you already searched it, but this is our standard protocol for anyone lost. We have to start at the center where the person disappeared. We don't mean to invade your privacy or anything."

I wave toward the house. "Please. I want you to."

Keith and Billy go first and then another ten members of the fire crew enter after them. Some of them are women with EMS patches on their sleeves. They all smile at me and then they spread out to search the house and both yards. They even go into the attic and basement.

I'm starting to understand why Chief Brewer said they didn't mean to invade my privacy. I get really uncomfortable when they go through every closet, box, and even look in the trash cans.

They do a much more thorough search and look in plenty of places I never would have thought of, but they still don't find Zeke.

They're still doing it when Chief Brewer goes out onto the sidewalk to have a powwow with the Police officers. Another five squad cars show up and the Police officers start canvasing the neighborhood and going door to door.

Chief Brewer comes back with a clipboard, a radio, and his phone. He finds me in the living room where I hug my arms over my body and pace back and forth.

Having all these people search for Zeke makes me feel so much worse. All these emergency crews confirm in my mind that he really is gone. He's lost. What if I never get him back? What if something really bad happened to him?

Keith and Billy come downstairs just then and rendezvous with Chief Brewer in the living room.

"He definitely isn't in the house or either of the yards," Keith reports.

"There's a gully behind the back fence with a little stream running down the drain into the city sewer system," Billy adds. "We searched the stream and the drains. He isn't down there and the grate over the sewer system is welded into place. He couldn't have gotten in there. Wherever he is, he's on land."

I pass my hand across my forehead. "Thank God!"

"You said you just moved in," Chief Brewer asks me. "So your son doesn't know anyone around here?"

I shake my head. "We just pulled in about half an hour before I called the Police. He doesn't know his way around town."

"The school is right down the block," Keith points out. "He would have been able to see that from the curb. He might have gone down there to check it out."

"We'll send the Police to search it," Chief Brewer replies. "I don't want to split up the crew by sending anyone to do someone else's jobs."

Keith nods, and right then, a different firefighter walks in with Zeke. This guy hasn't been here with the others and he doesn't wear any protective gear. I only know this guy is a firefighter because he wears a matching blue T-shirt with the Fire Department logo on it.

He's younger than the others, but no less muscular and square-shouldered. He wears his straight dark brown hair cut short on the sides and longer on top. His bright dark eyes dart around the house. "What's going on?"

I rush Zeke and grab him in a hug. "Oh, my God! Where have you been? I was worried sick! I thought something awful happened to you." I crush him against me and turn to the young firefighter who brought Zeke home. "Oh, my God! Thank you so much for finding him! I can't thank you enough!" Then I turn back to Zeke. "Are you all right? Where were you? I looked everywhere for you! Are you hurt? Why didn't you tell me where you were?"

"I didn't do anything," he grumbles. "You don't have to treat me like a baby."

"He came over to my place next door," the young firefighter adds and turns to Chief Brewer. "What are you doing here? He wasn't lost or anything."

"Do you not see the fire truck and all the Police cars outside?" Billy points out. "We've been organizing a citywide manhunt for this kid! We were just about to call in the rescue chopper."

"Why? He just came over next door to see if any kids lived there. We were just sitting there talking."

Keith rolls his eyes, groans, and turns away. "Jesus, Danny! Can't you even take a day off work without getting into trouble?"

"What?!" Danny counters. "You don't have to get on my case about it. I was just sitting on my couch minding my own business when he showed up. What's the big deal? I brought him home as soon as I realized his mother didn't know where he was."

Chief Brewer turns to me. "You'll have to excuse my brother, Ma'am. He has a tendency to wind up in the wrong place at the wrong time."

"How could I be in the wrong place at the wrong time when I was sitting on the couch in my own living room?" Danny asks.

"He has a Commendation for Heroism and a Medal of Valor," Zeke interjects. "It seems like he winds up in the right place at the right time."

Keith groans again. "Not that again!"

I turn Zeke around and hold onto his shoulders. I have to stop myself from shaking him. "You can't just disappear like that! We've talked about this! You have to tell me when you're going off on your own."

"Okay, okay," he grumbles. "I heard you. You didn't have to call the Police! God, Mom!"

"He just came over to check out the place," Danny cuts in. "Then we started talking and he had a sandwich. I'm sure he didn't mean to stay gone so long."

A few of the female paramedics come in to give Chief Brewer their reports. "All the windows upstairs are locked," a short, curvy woman with sandy brown ponytail tells him. "He couldn't have gotten out that way."

"You can call off the search," he replies. "The boy came home on his own."

"Or *not* on his own," Keith growls.

Chief Brewer pretends not to hear him. "Round up the crew. We're shipping out to the firehouse. I'll catch up with you once I clear the scene with the Police Department." He gives Danny a hard look. "You can go home now. I think you have some reading to do on your Professional Development course."

Keith snorts. "You bet he does. How's it coming along, little bro?"

Danny makes a face. "Shut up."

Chief Brewer turns to me. "Sorry about all that, Ma'am. Have a good day. I'm glad he came home safely."

"Thank you," I exclaim. "I'm so sorry about the inconvenience. I shouldn't have called you."

"Of course you should have and it's no inconvenience. That's what we're here for. Have a good one and don't hesitate to call if you need anything."

He bumps his knuckles on Danny's shoulder and gestures for Danny to leave with the rest of the fire crew.

He hesitates and holds out his hand to Zeke. "It was great to meet you. I'll see you around."

Zeke lights up when he shakes Danny's hand. The chemistry between these two is off the charts. "Could I come over again sometime, Danny? You can tell me some more of your stories."

"No!" I snap and try to get myself under control. "I'm sure the neighbors don't want you dropping in on them unannounced. I don't want you bothering everybody....."

"He wasn't bothering me—not at all." Danny turns back to Zeke and grins at him. "You can come over anytime you want. You can leave the gate open and consider my yard your yard."

"That isn't necessary...." I try to tell him.

"I know it isn't necessary. It would be a pleasure." He holds out his fist to bump Zeke's. "I'll see you around, buddy. Take it easy."

Then he walks out of the house with the rest of the crew.

Chapter 4:
Danny

"Did you finish your Professional Development course yet, Danny?" Brooke Elsworth calls across the firehouse break room.

"Did you even start it yet?" Ellis Barrett adds and everyone laughs.

"Very funny," I counter. "I can't be the only one who hasn't finished it."

"How far into it are you?" Billy Cates asks. "Then we'll know who's the farthest behind."

"Why is my Professional Development course now the topic of everyday conversation?" I ask.

"Because you're a slacker," Keith tells me.

"Because we need someone to make fun of," Chris Daniels adds.

"Because we have nothing else to talk about," Andy Skinner finishes.

"You must not if this is as interesting a topic as you can come up with," I reply. "What about that partial decapitation call we had day before yesterday?"

"Day before yesterday is ancient history," Keith points out.

"And my Professional Development course isn't?"

"Not if you haven't finished it, it isn't. If you had finished it, it would be ancient history and then we would have nothing left to talk about. We would find some other poor dope to make fun of."

"Like me," Ellis chimes in. "You don't how nice it is that the crew is making fun of someone else for a change."

I frown at him. "Did *you* finish the course?"

"Oh, sure. I finished it about three days after John assigned it to us."

My jaw drops. "No, you didn't."

He nods. "I took it home and knocked it out of the dang park, brother. Got the certificate and everything to prove it." He sighs, kicks back, and laces his fingers behind his head. "Now I don't have to think about it ever again."

I turn bright red and look away. "Crap."

"So how far into it are you?" Chris asks me.

I stand up from the couch. "I don't want to talk about it."

I'm just about to walk out of the break room and go hide in the garage where I can be alone.

Just then, my sister-in-law Leila, Keith's wife, strolls in. She's scheduled for the next shift. She's here because my crew's shift is almost over.

"Hey, sweetie," she tells me. "How's the Professional Development course coming along?"

The others laugh. "It isn't," Keith tells her.

Leila's eyes widen and she looks back and forth between us. "It isn't?"

"How about we lock you in one of the lockers downstairs until you finish it?" Billy suggests.

Just then, Caleb Watts rolls in for the next shift, too. "What are you masochists still doing here? Don't you all have homes to go to—or are we going to have to open the Home for Lost Firefighters to take care of you all?"

More laughter breaks out and everyone stands up to head for the door. Thank the stars no one is talking about Professional Development anymore.

I really need to take a lesson from Ellis. He always clowns around the firehouse and no one takes him seriously, but if he can get his course done that fast, I should be able to, too.

Something always comes along to get in the way, though. I really just need to go home tonight, sit down, and hammer it out like he says. I've been putting it off for way too long.

Everyone goes downstairs to the locker room where we meet up with Jacob Franks, Sophie McNish, Vince Jaeger, and Drew Killian who are also going on shift with Leila and the others right now.

Everyone talks at once and I get lost in the commotion. I grab my duffel bag and head out to the garage with the others before we all split up to go home.

We joke and make fun of each other on our way to the parking lot. I get into my pickup and make up my mind again. I won't do anything tonight until I finish my Professional Development course. Then I can relax.

I fire up the ignition and turn the truck out onto the street to drive home. I spot Chris driving away and wave to her. She turns in the other direction and I set off toward my own neighborhood.

The instant I turn in that direction, I spot Zeke Montgomery playing on the jungle gym at the school. It's Monday afternoon, so he must have started school today. Good for him. A kid as friendly and easy-going as he is will meet people and make friends in no time.

It must be hard for him to be an only child. I would have hated that growing up. I always had my brothers.

I smile at the sight of him. He's a good kid. I'm glad he moved in next door to me. It will be as nice for me to have him around as it will be for him to have other kids to play with.

I drive past him and wave, but he doesn't see me. He's too busy playing and sliding down the slides.

I happen to glance in my rearview mirror and all those good feelings fly out the window when a car pulls up to the school sidewalk. Two guys get out and start talking to Zeke on the playground.

I instantly get a bad feeling about it, but I'm already driving away from the school. I make a snap decision, yank my truck around the next corner, and drive around the block.

The guys are still there when I get there. They stand at the bottom of the slide talking to Zeke while he sits at the top. He doesn't slide down because they're standing too close at the bottom. He's too smart to put himself that close to them.

Now I know for certain that something is wrong. I slam my foot on the emergency brake, skid the truck to a halt, and climb out of the cab. I cross the playground in a few seconds. These idiots better not be messing with Zeke.

Before I can get there, one of the guys climbs up the ladder behind Zeke. The guy gets closer from behind. Zeke glances over his shoulder. Now he's trapped.

He kicks off and slides down. He tries to spring off the slide before he gets to the bottom, but the second guy leaps forward and catches Zeke before he can get clear.

Zeke kicks and struggles. The guy wrestles him back toward their car waiting at the curb. No damn way. No way in hell are these assholes gonna snatch some kid off the damn playground.

I pick up the pace, but I'm too far away to get there in time.

The guy rips open the back passenger door, hurls Zeke inside, and slams the door to lock him in. Zeke attacks the door and pounds the window with both fists.

The kidnapper dives into the driver's seat and fires up the engine. His friend races over and hops into the front passenger seat just as I make it over there.

They're just about to burn rubber and drive off with Zeke trapped in the back seat when I sprint in front of their car. I slam my hand on the hood to stop them from going anywhere and the driver hits the brake.

"Hey!" the driver yells through the window. "Get the hell out of the way!"

I point at him through the windshield. I can't remember ever being this mad in my life. "Don't you fucking move, you piece of shit! You stay right where you are and wait for the Police to haul your fucking ass to jail, you filthy, stinking cocksucker!"

I storm around the car, yank open the rear passenger door, and I have to get my temper under control when I pull Zeke out.

He scrambles over to me and I push him behind me as the two guys get out of their car.

I feel Zeke huddling behind me as I push him backward toward the school. I keep my body positioned between him and the two guys.

They both storm up to me. "Hey, asshole!" the driver bellows. "What the hell do you think you're doing?!"

I hold out one arm to make sure Zeke stays behind me, but he doesn't need any help. He cowers here holding onto me.

"That's right, you worthless pieces of shit!" I rage. "Come on! That's right! Move away from the car so the Police will be sure to find you trying to kidnap some kid off the goddamn school playground! You fucking lowlifes! You deserve to spend your lives behind bars!"

"He's our kid, you freak!" the second guy fires back.

"You think so?" I whip out my phone. "I'm sure his mother would have something to say about that. Let's call the Police and find out."

I quickly tap out 911 and get the dispatcher on the line. "911 emergency dispatch," she announces. "Please state the nature of the emergency."

"Two halfwits just tried to kidnap a kid from the Howe school playground," I blurt out. "We need about five squad cars and a paddy wagon—and maybe the SWAT team."

The two guys exchange glances. I keep a close watch on them while I give the dispatcher the school address.

The morons are still standing there when we hear sirens in the distance. I swear I'd tear them both apart if the Police weren't on their way right now.

The guys hesitate a little longer, but when the sirens get louder, they scramble into their car and hit the high road. Bastards. I make sure to give the dispatcher their license plate number before I hang up.

I spin around, grab Zeke, and pat him down all over. I can't stop my heart from pounding. "Are you okay?! Did they hurt you anywhere?! Are you all right?! I got here as fast as I could! Are you all right?!"

He nods fast and he's having trouble breathing, too. "I'm...okay... ..I'm....okay....."

"Did you know those guys?!" I realize I'm talking way too loudly. I might even be yelling at him, but I'm so hyped up on adrenaline that I can't slow down.

He shakes his head. "I never saw them before. They just showed up out of nowhere."

The Police roll in just then, but when they try to separate me and Zeke, he holds onto me and flies into a hysterical frenzy to stay with me.

"We need to take your statement," one of the officers tells me.

"Then take it," I tell him. "You can do that here, can't you?"

The guy sighs and starts writing down my statement. I get halfway through it before John shows up in his Fire Department support truck.

He takes one look at Zeke holding onto me and then John stands aside and listens in silence while I tell the officer what happened.

The officer finishes taking my statement and turns to Zeke. "Your turn, son."

"You should wait until his mother is present before you take his statement," I point out. "Don't you have rules about not questioning a minor without the consent of his legal guardian?"

The officer makes a face, but just then, Emily Montgomery shows up. I know her name because I had to give a statement to the Police about Zeke coming over to my house—plus I had to give John an incident report about it.

She can't be more than twenty-five, which means she had Zeke when she was less than eighteen. She's really pretty with a small, round face, curly brown hair with golden highlights, and voluptuous curves all over.

She wears jeans and a Midwestern-girl-next-door-style plaid button-down shirt. Her clothes show off every curve just in case I wasn't quite sure what might be hiding underneath.

She charges us, grabs Zeke, and nearly has a heart attack when she hears about what happened. She interrogates him, and when he tells her his side of the story, the officer writes everything down as fast as he can.

She hugs him again and I see him starting to get uncomfortable. I'm starting to understand why he thinks she's overprotective—not that I blame her.

She barely looks at me when she says, "Thank you so much! You're a lifesaver."

"It was nothing," I tell her.

"Are you okay?" John asks me. "You didn't get into it with the guys, did you?"

"No, but I would have. They only left because they heard the sirens."

"Maybe you'll get another Medal of Valor for this, Danny," Zeke tells me.

"Naw," I tell him. "This was nothing."

"Thank you. Really!" Emily insists. "I don't know how to thank you for....everything. I don't know what I would do if anything happened to him."

"It's no big deal," I tell her. "I'm just doing my job."

She makes eye contact with me for a split second and turns away again. "Come on, sweetie. We gotta go home."

"Just a minute, Ma'am," the officer tells her. "I just need to ask him a few more questions. Can you think of any reason why these guys might want to snatch your son in broad daylight?"

"You can ask us any questions you want another time," she counters over her shoulder. "You can contact me and I'll bring him to the Police station if you really need me to. We aren't doing it now."

She walks away with her arm around his shoulders. He shoots me a glance and then she hustles him away.

She gets him as far as the sidewalk before *she* shoots me a fleeting glance over her shoulder, too. Then she turns her back on us and hurries away toward her house.

Now I have no option but to face John. I expect him to read me the riot act about getting mixed up in this again, but he only cocks his head to study me.

"Is there anything you want to tell me?" he asks.

"Huh? No! I'm telling the truth. I was just driving home from work when I saw those guys. What was I supposed to do—drive on past and let them take him?"

"Of course not. You did the right thing. I'm proud of you."

"Then what's the problem?"

"There isn't one."

"Don't go making it out like I went looking for trouble or anything," I go on. "It wasn't like that at all."

"I wasn't going to say that."

"Then what are you trying to say?" I demand.

He shrugs. "Nothing. Are you busy tonight?"

I shuffle my feet. He really knows how to get under my skin. "I was going to work on my Professional Development course. I was on my way home from my shift to do it when this happened."

He only nods. "Okay."

"What?!" I counter. "What did I do this time?"

"Nothing. Do you want any help with the course?"

Now I know I have to get out of here. "No. I can handle it."

"Okay. Let me know if you do need help. That's what I'm here for." He claps me on the shoulder. "Have a good evening. If you finish, you can come over to our place for dinner. We'd love to have you."

He heads back to his truck and leaves me seething on the sidewalk. Now I won't be able to work on the course at all. I'll be too distracted by everything that just happened.

Chapter 5: Danny

I flip the pages of the Professional Development booklet on my dining room table, but as I suspected, I can't concentrate on anything.

I keep going over the confrontation at the playground. I can't stop every detail from repeating in my mind.

The officer is right. Those guys didn't just show up out of the clear blue sky to grab any kid they could catch off the playground. Is there some other reason why Emily is so protective of Zeke?

My mom would have waited for hours before she called the Police to report that one of her children was missing. She would have assumed we were playing around the neighborhood somewhere or at one of our friends' houses.

Then again, my mom raised me, John, and Keith. She's seen it all and knows better than to try to protect us from pretty much anything.

Emily is so young and she's on her own with a seven-year-old boy. Of course she's overprotective, but still.

She acts awfully jumpy where he's concerned and maybe she has a point about that. Is something deeper going on—something that would cause two strange creeps to steal Zeke from the playground?

I turn another page of my course booklet, but I haven't read a word of it in hours. Zeke should have been safe on the school playground.

Howe is a small town and everybody knows everybody—so who were those guys? Why did they go after Zeke of all kids?

None of it makes sense.....unless Emily is right and she really does have some reason to be worried about Zeke doing normal kid things. What could that be?

I turn another page. I really need to concentrate or I won't be able to show my face at the firehouse. I can't let Ellis beat me—but he already did beat me. There is no greater shame than that and I'm already living it .

Maybe I should have taken John up on his offer for help. Then again, I wouldn't get anything done if I went over to his place. He, Ellen, and their daughter Oakleigh would distract me even more.

Ellen and Oakleigh would probably give me a ration of shit about not finishing it—and don't even get me started on the crap I would have to endure if Keith was there, too.

I'm really not getting anything done here, but just as I'm about to give up, someone knocks on my front door. I check my watch. It's eight o'clock at night.

I go over there and stop dead in my tracks when I open it and find Emily standing on my porch. "Um.....hello," I greet her. "Is anything wrong?"

"Not at all. I wanted to give you this....to thank you for saving Zeke today." She holds out a ceramic baking dish covered in tin foil. "It's cannelloni with Italian sausage. I hope you like that."

"Really?! Thanks! I love Italian food." I take the dish. "This is great! Thank you."

"Well...." She rubs her hands together and looks over her shoulder. "I just wanted to thank you."

"Umm..... do you want to come in?" I glance toward her house. "Is Zeke okay?"

"He's fine. He's in bed....which is why I came over so late. I hope I'm not disturbing you."

"No, not at all." I wave toward the dining room table. "I wasn't doing anything important."

She squirms a little more. "I should probably get back. I don't like leaving him alone."

Those words send me straight back into detective mode. There's something going on with these two. I just need to find out what it is. "Come inside for a while," I tell her. "We're next-door neighbors. We should get to know each other."

"I shouldn't......" she begins again.

I hold the door open wider. "I'm gonna get really offended if you don't. Come on. He's either sound asleep or he'll be fine on his own for at least a few minutes."

I don't wait for her to answer. I walk back to the kitchen and put the baking dish in the fridge.

When I turn around, she's inside the house shutting the front door. I hastily fold up my Professional Development booklet and put it on the stack of paperwork at the end of the kitchen counter.

She creeps a little farther into the living room. "So....how long have you lived in this neighborhood?" she asks.

"About five years. All the cool people live in this neighborhood because it's near the school."

She blushes and looks away. "I guess that makes me one of the cool people."

"Of course it does. You have good taste buying that house. I couldn't figure out why no one bought it before. It's sweet."

"Yeah. It is." She beams at me. "I'm glad I'm not the only person crazy enough to see its charm."

"No way. It's gorgeous. The old couple who owned it last were still living in it when I bought *this* place. I would have bought that house myself if it had been for sale then. It's beautiful. It's so cozy and heart-warming."

She bursts into another grin and tries unsuccessfully to fight it back. "Yeah. I love it."

"So where did you move from? What made you decide to move to Howe of all places?"

She pretends to look away and spots my decorations on the mantel. "Oh, is this what Zeke was talking about with your Medal of Valor?"

"Let's not talk about that," I tell her and look away.

"Why not? You must be proud of them."

"I would be if they didn't make me a laughingstock at the firehouse."

She turns around fast. "Why are you a laughingstock?"

"Because they can't stop giving me endless grief about constantly saving the day. I can just imagine how it's going to go tomorrow when they find out what happened at the school."

She blinks at me in something like horror. "But what you did today was so....."

"Stop right there," I tell her. "Really. Don't talk about it. I already get enough crap about it as it is. Please. Just drop it. I just happened to be at the right place at the right time....."

Her eyes fall out of her head and I realize too late what I just said. I turn away and head back to the kitchen. "Do you want something to drink?"

"I shouldn't," she repeats. "I should get back."

"You haven't told me anything about yourself. What's the point of us getting to know each other if you don't tell me anything? Was Zeke in school before this? He seemed really starved for friends when he came over the other day."

She squirms even more and turns around to go back to the door. "I better go. It was nice talking to you....."

I dive across the room and just barely stop myself from grabbing her. "Emily! I meant what I said about Zeke being welcome to come over anytime....and you'd be welcome anytime, too. We're neighbors. If you need something, just holler at me over the fence. I could probably hear you from here."

She blushes, smiles, and looks away. "You're really nice. I didn't think people around here would be so nice."

I back off and raise both hands. "Hey! If you don't want to talk about yourself, that's fine. You can ask me anything about me. Do you want to know what it's like to have your older brother as your boss? I'll tell you. It's hell."

She tries not to laugh and does it anyway. "I kinda got that impression when he was here."

I start to relax. "And you don't want to know what it's like working with Keith."

Now she really does laugh. "Does he practice in front of the mirror to make himself look scarier?"

I join in the joke. "Come over here and sit down. You don't have to rush off."

I sit down on the couch. She hesitates and then lowers herself into an armchair across from me. She sits on the very edge of the seat like she wants to be ready to bolt in case I try something.

The way she acts confirms in my mind that something is wrong. Just in case I happened to have gone blind in the last few minutes, she glances toward the door to make sure her getaway is clear.

"Zeke's a great kid," I tell her. "You're doing an amazing job raising him on your own."

She turns bright red and looks the other way. "Thanks. He would be great even if I wasn't."

"No!" I tell her. "That kind of thing comes from the top. Trust me. I know."

"How do you know if you don't have kids?"

"I have plenty of kids in my life. John has a daughter and Keith and I babysit her all the time. Plus there are plenty of other kids in the firehouse family...."

"The what?"

"That's what we call our whole big extended family. John started it. We hang out together in our free time and have events together where we all just hang out and bond. We're all one big family. It's great. You should bring Zeke sometime."

Her eyes bug out again. I don't realize what I said to set her off, but all the color drains from her face and she launches herself to her feet. "I better go. It was nice talking to you."

I follow her to the door as fast as I can. She would bolt out into the night without even waiting for me to say goodnight to her.

"Is something bothering you, Emily?" I blurt out over her shoulder. "Are you in some kind of trouble? You should tell us if you are. We can help you."

"Us?" she asks without turning around. "Whoever you're talking about doesn't know anything about me and you're never going to." She grabs the door handle and yanks it open.

"I'm just trying to help, Emily. That's what I do. I can't seem to stop myself."

"Zeke and I don't need your help," she snaps over her shoulder.

"You could have fooled me," I say and immediately wish I hadn't.

She whips around so fast she nearly knocks me over. I expect her to go off on me big time, but instead, she just stares at me.

"Don't think I don't see it," I tell her. "I live right next door to you both now, so if there's a problem, I want to do something about it—kind of like I did at the school. I can't just turn a blind eye and pretend it isn't there when it is. You can't convince me that something isn't wrong."

She doesn't react. She just stands there staring at me. Now she's making *me* uncomfortable.

She finally sighs, passes her hand across her forehead, and her shoulders droop. "I just don't know...." she groans. "All this.....moving here.....and then those guys trying to take Zeke.....I guess it's all just kind of catching up with me, you know?"

"Let us help you. You don't have to do everything by yourself. John raised his daughter alone for ten years before he got married last year. Keith and I helped him every day. He couldn't have done it alone and neither of us wanted him to. That's what being family is all about."

"I wish I had that."

"Where is your family?" I ask and then raise my hands. "Don't answer that."

"They're....." She hesitates and then says, "They're in Ohio."

I raise my eyebrows. "That far? Why did you move away?"

She shrugs, but it's a defeated shrug. The tension drains out of her. "It's complicated."

"Well, if you want, I can pick up Zeke from school if you need me to.....or I can connect you up with some other parents at the firehouse. They always carpool and the kids stay over at each other's houses when their parents need them to. They have networks all over the neighborhood."

She looks up. "Really?"

"Yeah. Believe me. I've been in the middle of it for years. It can get pretty crazy sometimes with kids staying all over town. I swear I don't know how John did it all these years."

She stares at me in shock for a second and then, for no reason I can see, her eyes dart down to my mouth.

That glance takes me so much by surprise that I wind up glancing down at her mouth, too. She's really pretty. I noticed that about her right away, but the rest of her behavior made it clear that she was totally off limits.

That isn't why I'm interested in her. I'm just curious to know what's going on with her and to help her if I can. Helping her means helping Zeke. I would have to be a pretty worthless waste of a human being not to want to do that.

She looks back up into my eyes, and in that instant, I realize she *is* interested. Is that why she keeps so much distance between us?

Just thinking that and realizing it gives me another rush of adrenaline. What if.....?

I don't see anything about her that I wouldn't be interested in....and then there's Zeke. They're a package deal, but I don't see anything about him that I wouldn't be interested in, either. Is that why I acted so protectively toward him as the school?

I didn't think so at the time—or afterward. I didn't think of it at all until now.

She turns back to the door like she wants to leave, but it's too late. I've already seen that look and it takes me over.

She starts to open the door and my body acts on its own. I step up close to her, slip my arm behind her back, and pull her against me. The instant I do that, my body explodes in flames and a charge of heat rushes to my crotch. I want her.

I feel her body ignite at the same time and my crotch throbs against her. She shivers with tension and her eyelashes dip as the blood rushes to her cheeks.

I don't do anything for a second. I just hold her there where she can feel every thump of my heart beating through me and into her. She feels it. I know she does. She can't deny it when I hold our bodies sealed right up against each other like this.

I feel myself starting to get carried away. I can't do that. I need to take this slow. Whatever is going on with her, I don't want to scare her away—not any more than she already is.

I feel my heart pounding through my chest, too. Every inch of my skin burns for her. My senses heighten and I see her lips quiver with excitement. My mouth waters to kiss her and I feel her heart racing back at mine.

I flatten my hand against her back and let my hand slide just a little lower to the curve of her lower back. I press her hips into me just a little lower. Holy shit, she feels amazing!

She looks even more astonishingly beautiful like this. Her breasts heave against my T-shirt. From here, I can look right down inside her shirt buttons to her swollen cleavage where her bra pushes her breasts together.

I want to grab her. I want to feel every inch of her in my hands, but not yet. She isn't ready. I sense that without being told.

My breath catches in my nose. My body aches from all this fire burning me up. I'm going crazy for her.

That sound of my breath makes her look up. Her eyes aren't brown the way I thought they were. They're deep, deep green with brown and gold flecks.

They swim with drunken desire. Christ, she's beyond hot! I want to make her gasp and moan and scream while she looks at me with those eyes.

Some force outside myself makes me bring my other hand forward and I grab her hip. I want to grab her ass, but I stop myself in time and take hold of her hip instead.

I rock my swollen package between her legs and her lips sag open in a desperate moan. Her eyes float half-closed and her body sways in my arms.

Without thinking, I dive in and kiss her. As soon as our lips lock, I can't tear away. I devour her mouth and swirl my tongue around hers to taste every drop of her essence.

I ride her hips down on my spike and she squeals, but she doesn't pull away. She flexes her hips toward me and her hard pubic bone crushes me in a deep, pulverizing thrust. Oh, hell yeah.

I arch into her faster and harder. I grind into her, and in a flash, I turn her to the wall where I can crush her under my weight. Before I know what I'm doing, I'm driving between her legs and pushing her up the wall while I attack her mouth in ravenous fury.

She escalates just as fast. She doesn't hold back at all. She keeps spiraling her hips on my every move. Our rhythm synchronizes. Holy shit, I've never felt anything like this. This is beyond intoxicating. I can't hold back.

She claws at my chest and shoulders and back and hair. She bites my lips trying to kiss me even faster.

I throw caution to the wind and grab two handfuls of her beautiful, round, gorgeous ass to pull her legs around me.

She complies, and in a second, I'm pounding her against the wall through her jeans. She straps her legs around me yelping with every thrust. God, I want her so bad!

Her mouth drives me insane and I smell her perfume every time I inhale. I want to keep inhaling that forever. It sends me over the edge. I have to have her.

I tear her off the wall and stagger over to the couch still holding her around my waist. I only get as far as the back of the couch and manage to set her down on it. Now she's at the perfect height for me to drive into her.

I use my mouth to push her back and plunge my hand between her legs. I rub and crush her through her jeans. Her thighs crack apart and she moans in ecstasy. I feel her grinding on my hand. She wants it and I'm the one who's gonna give it to her.

I grab her jeans and tear her fly open. She attacks me ripping my shirt out of my belt and then my head explodes when her hands touch my bare skin.

I strip her zipper open and she has to get off the couch so I can pull her pants down. Neither of us can claw at each other fast enough.

She won't stop kissing me so I have to do everything by feel, but I don't care. I yank her jeans down to her thighs and then to her knees.

I push her back down on the back of the couch, drop on my knees, and her thighs fall apart for me to dive between them.

I get lost in her delicious scent and she whines in desire when I plunge my fingers in. She gushes into my mouth. I can't take much more of this. I need all of her. I can't wait a second longer.

Her fingers thread into my hair and she grabs fistfuls to pull my face into her harder. She rides my face in a frenzy building to an explosion. Her tissues swell and throb on my fingers.

I shut my eyes and fall headfirst into her depths. I'm in heaven. I can never get enough of this.

Her soft white thighs surround my face in so much bliss that I almost lose control of myself right there. I have to fight my body and mind under control. I'm gonna take her all night long and make her scream for me. I need to pace myself so I don't waste this moment for both of us.

She throws back her head and her body heaves with spasms. Her flesh trembles all around my face and then her muscles clamp on my hand as she bursts into broken screams.

She hurls herself down on my face and yanks my hair hard enough to hurt, but that only makes this so much better. I love the way she sounds and feels. I love the way she lets herself go for me.

Her screams die and soften to whimpers, but I don't stop. I ease off enough to tease her gently. She stays there rippling and swaying as the waves pass through her. Mmmm. She's so exquisite.

I give her a few more soft licks and pull my fingers out. I stand up raging hard. Now I have to have her.

Before I can move, she lunges away from me, yanks up her jeans, and runs out of the house. She leaves me standing there stunned and still smelling and tasting her in my nose and mouth.

Chapter 6: Emily

I charge across the lawn, down the street, and through my front door. I slam it behind me before I remember that I'm supposed to be quiet.

I gasp for breath, shut my eyes, and command my heart to stop pounding, but I can't settle down. I didn't just do that. I didn't just make out with Danny Brewer in his house next door.

Of course I did. His saliva and my juices soak my panties are soaked even now. God, he made me climax so hard! I've never climaxed that hard and we didn't even do it all the way.

I wanted to. That's the worst part. I wanted him more than anything. I would have done anything with him. That's why I had to stop it when I did.

I still feel his fingers plunging into me while he teases me to screaming rapture. I still feel his throbbing hard package drilling me against the wall. He's so incredibly hot—and that's nothing compared to how nice and kind and considerate he is.

God Almighty, why did I make out with him like that? I shouldn't have. Getting on bad terms with my closest neighbor would be the quickest way to spoil what's supposed to be a dream come true for me—and Zeke.

Zeke loves Danny. Zeke hasn't stopped talking about Danny since Zeke went over to Danny's house. Now Zeke thinks Danny is God's gift since Danny saved him at the playground.

I can't blame Zeke for thinking the world of Danny. Danny is pretty great. Okay, so he's more than great. He's a dream come true, too, but not for me.

He'll get himself someone who has their act together and that isn't me. Tonight was just a brief moment of relief for both of us. It will become a nice memory while we both move on with our lives.

He must have been just curious when he asked me all those questions about why I moved to Howe and where I moved from. He was just being neighborly like he said.

I drag my eyes open and have to concentrate to zip and button my jeans. Jesus, Emily! I really must be losing it if I just hooked up with my next-door neighbor.

At least I didn't hook up with him all the way. I would be really ashamed of myself if I did.

I'm ashamed of myself enough that I went that far. I shouldn't have. I'm a mother, for God's sake. I should control myself better and now I might have messed up a good thing for Zeke.

I finally calm down enough to listen, but the house sounds dead quiet. Zeke is still asleep. He never has to know I was gone. It would be a cold day in Hell before he ever finds out what just happened between me and Danny.

I creep upstairs and stop outside Zeke's bedroom to listen. He lies under the window with moonlight shining on him. My precious boy. I won't let anything happen to him.

I go into my own bedroom, sit down on the bed, and try to get my brain working in the right direction again. Everything feels blurry and indistinct after that massive orgasm Danny gave me.

I don't know if I have the mental capacity to take my clothes off and go to bed. I turn to the pillow and pull down the covers. Maybe I'll just lie down and go to sleep like this. I can't think clearly enough to do anything else.

I heave a giant sigh. I feel drunk and stupid.....and also incredibly good. I feel much more relaxed and at ease with myself than I have in years. I guess I really needed that.

I needed him to really give it to me even more. That would have really scratched my itch, but I'm not going there.

Just as I'm about to lie down and turn my brain off completely, my phone buzzes in my pocket. I pull it out. *Unknown caller.* That's weird. No one is supposed to have this number.

My thumb hovers over the answer button. I probably shouldn't, but maybe my mom got worried about me and Zeke. Maybe she tracked me down and just wants to hear that we're okay.

I answer it and immediately regret it when a husky male voice on the other end snarls, "I'm gonna kill you, Emily. I'm gonna find you and kill you for what you did to me...."

I throw the phone away from me before I think not to. It flies out of my hand on pure instinct to get that voice as far away from me as I can.

The phone hits the wall and then lands on the floor. It doesn't turn off and I hear the same voice laughing in a deep, throaty chuckle. It sounds like something out of a horror movie, but I can't bring myself to go over there to hang up.

He finally hangs up and the phone shuts off. It lies there, dark and asleep. The screen goes black. He isn't there threatening me or laughing at me for throwing the phone away—as if I could get away from him by throwing the phone away.

I leave the phone on the floor. I couldn't touch it now if my life depended on it.

I stretch out on top of the covers, but I keep my clothes on. All the fuzzy, good feelings of a minute before turn to cold sweat. I jump when I hear a cat yowling out in the neighborhood even though it's at least six blocks away. I can't shut my eyes for anything.

I lie there stiff and tense. I stare up at the ceiling trying to decide what to do. I can't get that voice out of my head.

I'm gonna kill you, Emily. I'm gonna find you and kill you for what you did to me.

Nervous anxiety makes my eyes dart across the ceiling, but there's nothing to see. I'm alone and Zeke lies asleep in bed down the hall. No one is here. No one is trying to kill me.

I force myself to shut my eyes, but when I do, I wind up thinking about Danny. He glares up at me from between my legs while his fingers drill me to the core. His mouth devours my lips while he pumps his body into me against the wall.

Does this mean I'm a shameless tramp when I should be a respectable single mother? I really need to get my life together instead of throwing myself at hot guys who just happen to look at me sideways.

I roll onto my side to try to get some sleep even though I know I won't be able to. What is wrong with me?

Just then, I hear what sounds like a rustle of dry leaves. It comes from down in the alley behind the house where I keep the trash cans and recycling bins.

I open my eyes and see what at first looks like Police emergency lights flashing outside. That can't be right. I didn't hear any sirens.

I sit up to take a look and my heart drops when I see flames licking up the house wall right under my window. In seconds, they woof up as far as my room and I get a powerful whiff of gasoline.

I stagger away from the window and trip over the bed before I charge out of the room. I dash into Zeke's room, but on the threshold, I look back.

My world comes crashing down around my ears when the big bay window by my bed smashes in. Flames dive through the opening and then my whole beautiful, magnificent bedroom goes up in flames.

I plunge into Zeke's room and grab him out of bed. "Get up, sweetie!" I yell over the noise of crashes. "Get up! We gotta get out of here!"

He takes a second to wake up enough to realize what's going on. "Mom?" he rasps.

I gather him in my arms and hug him way too tight. "Hold onto me, sweetie! Don't let go!"

I turn back to the hall, but just as I get to the door, another colossal thump of flame ejects down the hall coming from my room. Something like a monstrous dragon coils down the hall and blistering heat sears my cheeks. A powerful stench of gasoline stings my eyes and makes me choke

Zeke screams in my ears. He's wide awake now and his arms and legs clamp around me in a crushing hold. At least he's here where I can hold onto him.

I stumble back into the room and look all around me. I can't get out through the hall. That leaves one place left to escape from this inferno.

I turn to the window, but just then, the ceiling above my head explodes and broken, burning timbers collapse on top of me. I buckle to the floor holding onto Zeke for dear life.

"MOM!!" he shrieks in my ear.

I want to reassure him, but I can't see any way out of this house. We're trapped here with no way to escape.

Chapter 7: Danny

I stand in my living room staring at the closed front door. Emily isn't here anymore. I sure wish she was.

She leaves me out of my mind with desire, but something more than that is missing. I want more than that.

She still doesn't come back, so I pick up my fallen T-shirt and head upstairs. So much for getting my Professional Development course done. I'll be taking it on the chin tomorrow. Oh, well.

I go to my room and change into my pajama pants, but I don't put on a shirt. I stretch out on top of the bed, but I'm too wired to sleep. My body aches for her and I see her body undulating and shivering on my mouth.

I shut my eyes and let myself drift into that fantasy. My crotch throbs when I think about pushing her up against the wall.

She responded so beautifully. I want to do it all again....and again ....and again....and again. I never want it to end.

Her smell and taste drive me out of my mind and I let my hand drift down to my waistband. I start to get hard again thinking about her. How am I supposed to get her out of my mind?

My stomach tenses when I start touching myself. Mmmm. I can imagine all the ways I would have taken her if she hadn't run off like that.

I would have brought her up to this room, undressed her, and enjoyed every inch of that voluptuous body all night long. I would have stayed awake and worn her out in every possible way.

Or maybe I would have taken her over to her place so she would be able to get up and get Zeke ready for school tomorrow morning. I don't want to interfere with her obligations.

I want all of that. I want to be the man in her bed while she takes care of Zeke. I want to help them both. I want to be there all the time—or have them here. It doesn't matter to me as long as we're together.

That fantasy takes over. It excites me more than anything we did downstairs. I let it carry me away, but just as I'm letting myself disappear into it, I hear a crash outside.

I shoot off the bed and listen. I want to lie down again and finish this, but just then, I catch sight of something moving by my window.

I go over there to see what it is and my blood runs cold when I see Emily's house consumed in flames. The whole back side of it is involved by now—the side where Emily's bedroom is.

I charge downstairs without putting on a shirt or shoes. She better not be in there—but where else would she be? Zeke is in there, too.

That thought gives me all the energy I need to race over to her place. I didn't bring my phone, but there isn't time to call anyone anyway. Hopefully the neighbors will do it, but right now, I have to find a way into that house.

I charge through the gate and circle to the side where the master bedroom looks out over the backyard. Flames block out the destroyed bay window. The whole master bedroom is gone and the whole place reeks of gas.

I circle to the backyard. At least I can breathe fresh air here, but I still smell the fumes. They envelop the house in that choking smell.

There has to be a way inside. I remember Sophie saying that Emily keeps all the windows locked on the top floor, but I don't care about that. I can't let a minor detail like that stop me. If even one of them is alive in there, I have to get them out. I'm the only one who can.

I stop next to a trellis twined with roses climbing up to one of the top-floor bedrooms. The thorns look three feet long from here, but that's the price I'll have to pay.

I leap onto the trellis and jab my hands and feet on the thorns. They tear my pajama pants and cut into my skin, but I hardly feel it.

I get all the way up to the window and see flames licking into the small bedroom beyond. The roof is starting to collapse. Emily crouches on the floor holding Zeke in a death grip.

I punch out some of the windowpanes and gash my knuckles, but the frame turns out to be stronger than I expected. I have to crane my foot back and kick the window frame in.

Scorching hot air blasts out into my face and burns my cheeks and eyelids. I roar in pain, but I have to get into the room. Blasts of gas fumes make the smoke and heat even worse.

Emily keeps her head down as falling timbers rain on the bed and carpet. She doesn't see me and neither does Zeke.

I knock out as much of the glass as I can and climb into the room, but I cut myself on that, too. I feel myself bleeding, but I'll worry about that later.

Gas fumes choke the room. I spring over to Emily. "Come on!!" I bellow. "Come with me now! We're getting out of here."

She looks up at me with huge eyes. Maybe she doesn't even recognize me. I pull her to her feet. Zeke won't unwind his arms and legs from her for anything. That's okay. At least he's safe.

I tow her to the window. "You have to climb through and climb down the trellis! Hurry! Don't worry about the thorns! Just get down to the ground! Understand?!"

She nods fast. She's too shocked and terrified to speak or even blink. I kick out the rest of the glass and pry Zeke out of her arms. "Go! I'll bring him after you!"

She scrambles over the windowsill and lowers herself onto the trellis. Zeke latches onto me. His thin arms and legs wrap around my neck and body. He feels good holding onto me like this. I can protect him.

"It's gonna be okay, buddy," I murmur in his ear. "Everything's gonna be okay. I promise. I'm gonna get you out."

Emily starts climbing down, but before she can take her hands off the windowsill, another section of the roof buckles. Burning timbers crash down on top of me and Zeke.

I bend over just in time to take the blow across the back of my shoulders and the impact throws both me and Zeke down on the floor.

"ZEKE!!" she shrieks. "ZEKE!!"

I flounder to see what's happening. Burning beams angle all around me and the fumes make me dizzy. The timbers form a little cage around me and Zeke and block us from getting to the window.

I gather him in my arms and he grabs hold of me again, but not as tightly. He goes limp for a few seconds before he starts moving normally again, but he doesn't regain his former strength. He must have gotten hurt.

I clamp my arms around him. I'm gonna make good on my promise to him. I'm gonna get him out come Hell or high water.

I stagger back to the window and I have to climb over and under burning timbers to get there. Emily thrusts out one arm at me. "ZEKE!!" she howls.

"GO!!" I roar. "GET DOWN THERE SO I CAN GET OUT!! GO, EMILY!!"

She finally gets the message and climbs down sobbing her eyes out, but at last she makes it to the ground. I see blue and red lights flashing in the distance. Thank God someone is coming to help us.

I hold onto Zeke with one arm and climb out onto the trellis. I tear myself up even worse climbing down, but I really don't give a shit anymore. I have him and then my torn, bloody feet touch the cool grass.

I collapse and sprawl on my back with Zeke still holding onto me for all he's worth. I hear him crying in my ear and then Emily collides with us. She sprawls over both of us and bursts into racking sobs. She covers Zeke with hundreds of kisses and she won't stop touching him all over.

Then I hear Keith say, "Holy shit!" and the paramedics surround me.

"Can you open your eyes, Danny?" Chris asks me.

I try and she shines her flashlight in them one after the other. "How's your breathing?" Leila asks me.

"It hurts," I croak. "Zeke got hit in the head. He might have passed out for a second."

Leila takes hold of Zeke to pull him off me. "Come here, buddy. Let's take a look at your head."

She starts to pry him away from me, but he bursts to life and struggles out of her arms. "DANNY!!" he screeches. "DANNY!!"

"It's okay, buddy," I choke. "I'm here. I'm with you. I'll stay with you. Come on. Let the paramedics check you out."

I have to sit up, but I'm so torn up and exhausted that I slump as soon as I get upright. Chris puts an oxygen mask on my face, but when Leila tries to do the same thing to Zeke, he resists.

He jerks his head from side to side until I take it out of her hands. "It's okay, pal," I tell him. "See? I'm wearing one. It will help you breathe."

I put it on him, but he's too hysterical to think straight. He won't let go of me, which makes Leila's job harder.

Drew comes over to us and starts bandaging my hands and feet. Now all these cuts really hurt.

"Let's get you all transported," Leila tells me and touches me on my good shoulder. "Get on the gurney, sweetheart, and we'll load you into the ambulance."

I have to summon all my remaining strength to drag myself to my feet just long enough to sit down on the gurney. Emily flutters around us the whole time howling with sobs and trying to hug Zeke while he still holds onto me.

As soon as they get me onto a gurney, Leila tries again to put him onto another one where she can work on him. He goes crazy again and starts screaming for her to give him back to me.

"It's okay, buddy!" I yell over his screams. "I'm going with you! We're going to the hospital together! See? I'm going with you!"

I take him out of Leila's arms and lay him on the other gurney myself. He's completely insensible from fear and probably pain.

Keith and Billy have to wheel my gurney over to his so I can get right in his face and talk to him enough for them to strap him down. They restrain his arms to stop him from tearing his oxygen mask off.

As soon as they strap him in, his eyelids start to droop. "Danny!" he husks.

"I'm right here, buddy. I'll be with you all the way. Everything's gonna be all right. I promise you that."

His eyes sink the rest of the way. "His blood pressure is dropping!" Leila snaps. "We gotta go. Lie down, Danny."

I settle back on my gurney and now there's nothing for me to do but collapse while they take me to the hospital with Zeke and Emily.

They wheel me to the ambulance and load me and Zeke into the same unit. Just before they close the doors, I see Emily's house completely enveloped in flames. The fire crew doesn't even try to save it because there is no saving it.

They concentrate on the two houses on either side, one of which is mine.

Chapter 8: Emily

I sit slumped on the hospital bed and try not to notice the nurses, medics, and doctors bandaging and stitching up all the many cuts, gashes, scratches, and burns all over Danny's body.

He sits on a different bed across the same section of the emergency department. He wasn't wearing a shirt at the fire and he isn't wearing one now. He sits on the bed next to me where I have no choice but to see everything that's wrong with him.

A female paramedic with long dark hair and a metal leg brace stands behind him. She spreads some kind of gel across a huge burn on the back of his shoulders where that falling timber hit him.

"You really did a number on yourself this time, sweetheart," she tells him. "You're gonna have this scar for the rest of your life."

He snorts and doesn't look up. He flinches when she puts another dab of the gel on the burn. "Just bandage it so I can put my clothes on. I didn't come down here to show off my body to the nurses."

She laughs at him. "You know you did."

He doesn't take the joke. That's the second time tonight I've heard some female paramedic call him, "sweetheart".

Maybe he really does go through the nurses once a week. How would I know? I wouldn't be surprised considering the way all these women act.

She hobbles across the room, comes back with a huge square sheet of gauze, lays it across the burn, and presses it into the gel. "How's that?" she asks him. "Is it better now that the air can't get to it?"

"Yes," he mumbles over his shoulder. "Thanks, darlin'."

A few other nurses come over and start wrapping up his hands one after the other. The medics have already spent hours dealing with all the cuts and stabs to his feet. He wears two giant socks of gauze wrapped around both of them.

The medic with the leg brace starts taping the gauze to his back. He sits there hunched and stained with soot through the whole procedure. He occasionally glances in my direction and I immediately look away.

Zeke is upstairs somewhere getting treated for a head injury. I'll never forgive myself for him getting hurt. He could have died in that fire. I could have died in that fire. We both would have if Danny hadn't gotten us out.

The paramedic with the leg brace finishes taping the bandage to Danny's back, comes around in front of him, and shines a flashlight in his eyes. Then she stands back and looks very deeply into his eyes. "Are you sure you don't want some morphine? That one has got to hurt."

"Yes...I mean, no, I don't want any morphine."

She smiles at him. "Let me know if you change your mind."

She shoots me a glance and is just about to leave when Chief Brewer comes in with Keith. They look at me, too. Then they look at the paramedic and then they finally approach Danny.

"Are you okay?" Chief Brewer asks him.

Danny shrugs and doesn't look up.

Chief Brewer pats him on the side of the cheek and grips the back of his neck. "That's the pain talking. You'll heal from this and then you'll be back on the horse." He glances over at me again. "Where's the boy?"

"He's upstairs getting a CT on his head," the female paramedic replied. "Leila thought he might have some intracranial bleeding, but he just had a really bad concussion. He's gonna be okay."

I burst into tears at those words. I can't hold it back. I cover my mouth and turn my face away, but they can all see me breaking down right here in front of everyone.

Danny hops off his bed right away. He has to hobble on his badly injured feet. "Hey!" he murmurs. "It's okay! He's all right! Everything's gonna be okay."

He sits down on the edge of my bed, puts his arm around my shoulder, and kisses me on the side of the head. I can't even appreciate that he's being so kind. He always is, but that just makes me feel worse.

My boy. I almost lost him tonight. What kind of terrible mother am I to put my own child in danger like this?

Just then, two men come in and look around at everyone. Both of them are wearing business suits, but they also both wear Police Department badges hanging from their jacket pockets.

Both officers shake hands with Chief Brewer and Keith. Then the officer on the left says, "Hey, Ellen," to the paramedic with the leg brace.

"Hey, Jim," she replies. "How's it going?"

"Not so hot considering tonight's disaster." Both officers turn to me. Neither of them comments on Danny sitting here with his arm around me like we're a couple or something. "We need to take all your statements on the fire."

Chief Brewer steps over to the side of my bed where Danny is sitting. "Emily, this is Police Chief Jim Walker and Detective Eli Hill.

He's the detective sergeant at the Police Department who specializes in arson."

Detective Hill spins around to stare at him. "Are you sure it was arson?"

Chief Brewer nods and Keith chimes in. "The whole scene reeked of gas. You could smell it down the block."

Detective Hill turns back to me. "Did you smell gas, too, Miss Montgomery?"

I nod and struggle to pull myself together before I answer. "It....came through....the window.....when the glass shattered."

"No way could a house go up that fast without some kind of accelerant," Chief Brewer adds. "We'll do a full chemical screen in the morning, but there's no question. Someone set that fire and they deliberately set it to take the house up real fast."

"And it started right outside Emily's bedroom window," Danny adds. "Whoever did this tried to kill her, plain and simple."

Detective Hill takes out his notebook. "Well, Miss Montgomery? You wouldn't tell us anything about the men who tried to abduct your son from the school. Do you know someone who would burn your house down with you and your son inside it—someone who wanted to hurt you both?"

I can't take this anymore. I throw both hands over my face and a tornado of sobs breaks out of me. I feel like it will tear me in half any second now. It hurts as much as if it's tearing me in half even now.

"It's Colin, okay?!!" I howl. "He already tried to kill me twice before I ran away from him! He called my phone right before the fire started and said he was going to kill me for....."

No one says anything for a second. "Who is he?" Detective Hill finally asks.

"He's Zeke's father! We were married.....I mean.....we have been married for eight years. He kept me and Zeke locked up in the house and he tried to kill me in front of Zeke twice before I found a way to escape! He's been following me around the country ever since."

"Why didn't you report it?" Chief Walker asks.

"I did!!" I shriek. "I reported him five times in Cleveland, but the Police never did anything. You can ask Zeke if you don't believe me! He saw his dad attacking me right in front of Zeke. He's seen it all."

"Hey!" Danny murmurs. "It's gonna be all right!"

I squirm out of his arm. I can't stand the way he's touching me. All his attention and care drives home that I'll never be good enough for him. I'll never be good enough for anyone. "Leave me alone, Danny!" I wail. "It's not gonna be all right! Just leave me alone!"

I feel him stiffen, but before he can do or say anything, Keith takes hold of Danny's arm and pulls him off the bed. Danny resists and then Keith uses just a little more force to drag Danny away from me.

The feeling of Danny losing contact with me squashes my last shred of hope. He's been nothing but kind to me since day one. He's the one person in all of this that actually tried to help me and Zeke.

Danny didn't do that to get into my pants. I know that for certain. He helped Zeke that first morning and Danny wasn't even thinking about anything between us when he saved Zeke on the playground.

This whole thing is turning into such a disaster.

"So...." Detective Hill goes on. "Your son said he'd never seen those men on the playground. Is that true? Did he know who they were?"

"No," I moan. "Colin never sent anyone after us before. It's always been just him by himself."

Chief Brewer takes a step forward. He does it in a way that makes it painfully obvious to everyone that he's moving his big body between me and Danny.

"We'll get out of your hair so you can finish taking Emily's state-ment in private," Chief Brewer tells Chief Walker. "You can get in touch with us when you're ready to take Danny's statement. Come on, Ellen."

He and Keith turn away, but they stand guard over Danny to make sure he doesn't come near me again. He stands there looking at me for so long that Keith has to pull him away again.

I can barely stand to look at Danny. I see so plainly how much it hurts him that I'm pushing him away. He doesn't understand why......or maybe he does and that just makes it even more unforgivable.

Ellen follows them out of the room and shuts the door. Now I'm completely alone with these cops and I break down sobbing all over again. The one person who actually tried to help me—the one person who *did* help me—is gone.

I pushed him away. I told him to leave me alone. I really must be lost if I did that.

Chapter 9: Danny

I bend over the last page of my Professional Development course book and write in my answer to the last question. I've been working on it for an hour at the firehouse breakroom table.

Ellis comes over to me, leans close to my ear, and murmurs in a sing-song tone, "All around the cobbler's bench, the monkey chased the weasel....."

"Then you came along and took the monkey home for a good spanking, didn't you?" I mutter over my shoulder. "You can tell us. We all know the truth."

Laughter breaks out among the rest of the crew sitting around, but not even that distracts me from finishing this thing. I keep writing, but I have to stop when Keith comes up behind me.

He claps me on the shoulder, but like the good big brother he is, he makes sure to clap me on the shoulder that isn't injured. "This boy can get the job done when he wants to. You'll ace it, champ."

I don't look up. "Thanks, man. I appreciate the vote of confidence."

"You're the man." He gives me one last affectionate squeeze on the neck and goes over to the fridge.

He's just sticking his head into it when John comes in. "All of you get downstairs and do the hose inspection like I told you to this morning. Quit stalling. It has to be done by the end of the month, which is tomorrow. Go on." He spots me sitting there. "You can finish that later, slugger. Go downstairs with the crew and get it done."

"I won't have to finish it later because I just did." I fold over the last page and hold it out to him. "I'm done."

He raises his eyebrows at me. "No kidding? Good job."

"Don't sound so surprised." I stand up, push in my chair, and stick my pen into the arm pocket on my T-shirt. "You can let me know my score after we finish with the hoses."

He starts flipping the pages to read my answers. I head for the door to go down to the garage. I can already hear people laughing down there.

He shoots out a hand and grabs my arm to stop me. "Hey! If you need to take some more time off...."

"No, I don't. I don't want to." I try to pull out of his hold. "I'm here. I want to work."

"I don't want you to get your hands and feet wet—you know. I don't want anything to weaken the stitches....or anything."

"I'm fine. You don't have to worry about me....and I'll wear gloves over the bandages. Really. I'm here to work. I don't need to take any more time off. Seriously. I'll let you know if I need to."

I tug the rest of the way out of his grip and go downstairs before he can question me any further. I don't want to talk—to anyone about anything.

This whole thing with Zeke and Emily is really starting to get to me. It's been three days and I haven't seen or heard from either of them.

I've been trying to work a lot to take my mind off both of them. I knew something was wrong. Now I know what it is.

Now the cocksucker who did this to them is still running around loose out there. The asshole already tried to kill Emily multiple times. God only knows what he did to Zeke.

She already told me what he did to Zeke. This Colin creep kept them locked up in the house while he terrorized them both. He tried to kill Emily right in front of their own son. Who the hell does that shit?

I pull on a pair of latex medical gloves to cover my bandages and try one more hopeless time to throw myself into work, but nothing takes my mind off it. The rest of the crew keeps away from me. They joke with each other, but not with me—which on its own means something is wrong.

They all know not to screw with me when I get like this. I don't get mad very often, but when I do, it isn't pretty. They all give me a wide berth—except for Keith.

He goes out of his way to be nice to me and show me lots of affection. He's the only one who can come near me when I get like this.

That's his way of telling me that he understands. He knows why I'm so pissed off and he supports me. He doesn't think I'm a maniac for caring what happens to Zeke and Emily. Keith knows better.

He also doesn't act like I'm some kind of pervert for trying to get close to her when she told me to leave her alone. Sure, he was the one who pulled me away from her in the emergency room, but that's okay. He was just helping both of us. She was too upset to deal with me. I can understand that.

I will never understand or accept some fuckwit hunting down his terrified wife and son, trying to kidnap the poor kid from the God damn school playground, and then setting their house on fire with both of them inside it.

The jackass could have killed Zeke, too, for Christ's sake. This Colin really must be a psycho.

I start helping the crew lay out the hoses, but as soon as we get out onto the concrete driveway in front of the garage, my gaze wanders to the school. Is Zeke over there? Do the teachers even have a clue how much danger he's in?

What if his father tries something again—like coming to the school to pick up Zeke himself? The bastard could tell the teachers in all honesty that he's Zeke's father. They wouldn't be able to stop this freak from taking Zeke and driving off into the sunset.

I shudder at the thought. I can't just sit around and do nothing while Zeke and Emily might be in danger. I'm just not wired that way.

I turn back to the job and spot Keith watching me. I should talk to him. I should get his help. That's why he's acting all attentive and big-brotherly toward me. I should take him up on that. What the hell good does it do to have two older brothers if they can't come through for me in the clutch?

We finish the hose inspection and I help Keith and Billy write out the report to give to John. Then it's time to go home.

I head down to the locker room and get my stuff out of my locker. The rest of the crew horses around and shoots the bull on their way out to the parking lot.

I take a little longer changing into a fresh T-shirt. Sweating on the concrete driveway stings my burn, but who cares? The pain just makes me even more murderously furious at this Colin Montgomery asshole. Even the name makes him sound like the kind of guy who would be better off at the bottom of a deep canal.

By the time I change and shut my locker, I'm alone in the locker room. The second crew is already upstairs in the breakroom.

I have to carry my duffel bag since I can't put it over my shoulder. Getting injured is the worst.

I'm about to walk out the door when Keith and John roll up. Speak of the devil—two of them.

"Do you want us to go with you?" Keith rumbles.

I lower my eyes to the floor. "Yeah. I was just gonna come and ask you."

"Let's do it," John tells me. "Do you want to take my truck?"

"Let's take mine," I reply.

He only nods and we all go out to the parking lot. This feels good. I don't have to do this all on my own. I'm beyond grateful for their help and support. I couldn't ask for two better wingmen.

I drive back to my house first, but of course Zeke and Emily aren't there. Cordon tape surrounds the little that's left of their house. *Crime Scene—Danger—Keep Out,* the tape reads.

It's a crime scene if ever there was one. The accelerant screen has already come back with massive doses of octane all over the eastern side of the house where Emily's bedroom was. Both our reports and the reports of dozens of other witnesses confirm that the fire started there—right where it would put her in the most danger. The cocksucker.

The danger isn't the house anymore, though. It's out on the street. Zeke and Emily won't be safe anywhere until the Police put the bastard behind bars.

I drive into my own driveway, take one look at the cordon tape, and reverse back out onto the street. I've been seeing the charred remains of her house for three days. The wreckage doesn't tell me anything.

I skid onto the road and take off into town. First, we stop by the school and find out from the teachers that Zeke hasn't come back to school since the fire. He's vanished off the face of the earth.

"Head for the Police Department," John tells me from the passenger seat after we leave the school. "Emily must have given them a forwarding address where they could find her if they needed to clarify anything about her statement.”

I follow his instructions, but when we get to the station and track down Eli Hill, he won’t tell us anything. “Sorry, fellas,” he tells us. “The case has a domestic hold on it.”

“What the hell is that supposed to mean?” Keith growls.

“It means the victim’s contact details are under seal by a protective order. It’s supposed to stop the perp from doing exactly what you boys are trying to do right now—find the victim. I couldn’t give you her forwarding address even without the protective order. That’s confidential. You should all know better than that.”

“Don’t you realize how much danger she’s in?” I counter. “The asshole already tried to kill her twice before. This is the third time.”

He holds up his hands. “Sorry. I can’t help you. If we question her again, I can tell her you’re looking for her. That’s the best I can do.”

I open my mouth to argue some more, but my brothers pull me away. This is why I need them with me. They can see this case so much more clearly than I can.

“We’ll check the hospital next,” John tells me on our way out of the building. “Ellen can tell us if Zeke is still in the hospital.”

“He isn’t,” she tells us when we roll up to the ER. “He got released the same night you brought him in. It’s like I told you. He had one hell of a concussion.”

“It would have been more than that if he passed out from the blow,” I counter.

“They aren’t here. That’s all I can tell you.”

“Did she leave a forwarding address?” John asks.

“Did she leave any address at all?” I cut in. “Her damn house just burned down. It isn’t like she could give you her real address.”

She studies me for a second and then turns back to the nurse's station where she's sorting out the patients' charts. "I could get in a lot of trouble for this, but because it's you, I'm gonna throw you a bone."

"Tell me anything," I insist. "I don't care what it is."

"The address she left is the homeless shelter on the corner of Howe Avenue and Chestnut Street. She called a cab to take her there straight from the hospital when the doctors released her and Zeke. I'm guessing she has nowhere else to go."

John, Keith, and I go back out to the truck, but I'm too disturbed to drive. I get into the passenger seat while Keith drives. I'm too consumed with my own dark thoughts to say a word on our way downtown.

What the hell is Emily doing taking her injured son to a homeless shelter? Then I remember. She's running for her life from some murderous lunatic who doesn't care who he kills.

She just lost her house. She ran away from Colin to save herself and Zeke. She probably doesn't have much money.

Damn it. I shouldn't have left the hospital when Keith and John took me out of the room. I should have stayed there to make sure she had a place to stay. This is all my fault. I should have done more to help her.

Keith parks outside the shelter. I sit in the passenger seat seething in buried agitation for a long time. I even forget that my brothers are here.

John finally breaks the silence. "You go in and talk to her. She won't want to see us all roll up on her. You can let us know what you want us to do once you talk to her."

I take a deep breath and get out. I'm so jumpy that I forget to thank John and Keith for this. They know what's important and they know I have to face Emily alone.

I check in with the reception desk. The receptionist gives me a big song and dance about telling me where Zeke and Emily are. I have to repeat over and over that I'm not checking into the shelter for the night. I'm just here to talk to them—that's all.

I make such a stink about it that the receptionist calls the manager to deal with me. She takes one look at the Fire Department logo on my shirt and tells me right away where I can find Emily.

I walk into a huge room lined with dozens of beds in rows. People who haven't showered in years sprawl on the beds. Some of them snore. Others reek of liquor. Emily is NOT staying here with Zeke. No way in hell.

I spot them across the room. They occupy two beds in the far back corner away from everyone else. Zeke and Emily sit on their separate beds talking to each other with their heads together.

I walk over to them and come up behind Emily. She's so busy talking to Zeke that she doesn't see me.

He does. His eyes pop open and he lunges off the bed to hug me. "Danny!"

I hug him back, but I watch her to see her reaction to my sudden arrival. "Hey, buddy," I tell him. "How's the head?"

"It hurts a lot." He sits back down, beams up at me, and then his expression darkens when he sees the bandages on my hands. "Are you okay?"

"I'm fine. I was just worried about you two." I sit down on Emily's bed and turn to face her. I pretend not to notice her cringing to pull away from me.

"What are you doing here?" I ask her. "You could have stayed at my house."

"No, we couldn't," she murmurs, but she won't look at me. "I don't want to impose on you after everything you've already done for us."

"I haven't done anything for you!" I snap. "You can't stay here! Zeke got a really bad head injury during the fire. You need a real place to stay. Jesus! Look at this place! You are NOT staying here, Emily! Are you trying to offend me?"

"Of course not. It's just...."

I grab her hand. "Come on—both of you. Get your stuff. You're coming home with me right now. Don't argue. Just come on."

She pulls her hand out of mine. "You don't understand. It isn't like that between us."

"I don't give a damn what it's like between us. I wouldn't let my dog stay here. Now will you stop arguing and come on? This place is terrible."

"Come on, Mom," Zeke whines. "Please can we? I hate this place. It makes my head hurt."

She glances at him and then her eyes dip back to the floor. She has to know this place is no good for him—for either of them.

I don't want to know why she didn't just ask me in the first place. She better not think it's because we made out that night. That better not be the reason—as if that would make a difference.

I don't even care about making out with her. If she needs help, she's gonna get it. If she's too uncomfortable around me, then I'll make sure she gets the help she needs from someone else.

"All right," she finally murmurs. "Just give us a minute to get our stuff and check out for the night."

"Great." I have to stop myself from kissing the side of her head again. I really want to, but she obviously doesn't want that. "I'll be right back. I just need to fold down the seat in the cab of my truck."

I go back out to the parking lot where John and Keith lean against the truck fender talking.

"How did it go?" John asks.

"Yeah, it's all good. They're coming with me now, so......"

"We'll disappear." Keith hands me the keys. "Take 'em home."

"Are you sure you don't need a ride or something?"

"We'll take care of ourselves," John tells me. "You concentrate on taking care of them. Call us if you need us."

He and Keith push themselves off the truck and set off walking across the parking lot. They really would walk all the way home just to make Emily think I came here alone. Those are my brothers. They're both as solid as rock and I love them for that.

I have a job to do here and I don't have to fold down the seat in the truck cab because John was just sitting on it. The truck is ready to go, but Emily doesn't need to know that.

I go back inside just as they're collecting their stuff. They have almost nothing since all their worldly possessions got burned in the fire. That Colin really is the scum of the Earth. He better hope I never get my hands on him.

Chapter 10:
Emily

I can't look at Danny on our way out of the homeless shelter. I can't look at anyone else, either. This is the most ashamed I've ever been in my life. I'm more ashamed of this than the fact that I married a violent monster who's been trying to kill me for years.

I can't believe I actually let all of this happen—not just to me, but to my son. I nearly got him killed. Now I made him stay in a homeless shelter for three days.

Zeke bursts into a huge grin when we walk out to the parking lot and he sees Danny's pickup truck parked there. Danny tries to fight back the urge to grin at Zeke, too, but those two are cut from the same cloth. Jesus, what have I gotten myself into?

Danny puts our few bags in the truck bed. Then he folds the front seat forward so Zeke can climb into the back.

Then Danny holds the passenger door open for me. I catch him looking at me like *that*—like he's being a gentleman holding a lady's door open for her.

I look away. I don't want him thinking of me like that—any of it. I don't want him trying to treat me with respect when that's the last thing I deserve.

The simple fact that I need his help makes me feel even more like the loser I am. I should have been able to take care of Zeke on my own. I should have been able to rent another house or a motel room or something—anything other than winding up on the street with a seven-year-old kid and no way to take care of him.

Danny gets behind the wheel, fires up the engine, and starts driving across town. Zeke talks Danny's ear off the whole time about the fire, the hospital, the guys from the playground, and the Police questioning him and taking his statement about both incidents.

Then Zeke grills Danny about everything the fire crew has been doing and everything Chief Brewer is doing to prove that the fire was arson.

"It isn't really a question," Danny tells him. "The gas fumes were suffocating. We all smelled it, but he needs to do chemical analyses to document it for the Police investigation."

"It's so cool that your brother is the fire chief," Zeke exclaims.

"Yeah, John is the man. My other brother Keith is our most senior firefighter. He's basically in charge when John isn't around. Then it goes down the ranks from there. I think Billy Cates and Leila Cunningham might be tied for next senior."

Zeke frowns. "I thought you were one of the guys in charge."

Danny laughs. "No, I'm not. I'm somewhere in the middle. Keith is older so he's been doing it longer. That's why he's higher-ranked."

"But you have more decorations than him....don't you?"

Danny's cheeks flush. "I can't remember how many he has, but you don't rise in rank by getting decorations. You rise in rank by being responsible enough to take charge and tell the other firefighters what to do when John isn't around."

"Wow," Zeke breathes. "It's so complicated."

"You want to see complicated? You should see some of my Professional Development books. I have them at home. You can see them when we get there."

Zeke brightens right up. "Cool! I want to know everything!"

Danny glances over at me before he goes back to looking at the road in front of him. I cringe at their conversation. No way is Zeke going to become a firefighter.

I should discourage him right now so he doesn't start getting ideas, but I don't want to do that in front of Danny. That really would offend him.

I couldn't stand knowing that Zeke was going into burning buildings and getting hurt the way Danny does. Danny is a hero and everything, but I don't want Zeke doing stuff like that. I would have a heart attack. God only knows how his mother handles it with three sons all in the fire service.

He pulls up in front of his house and Zeke goes silent when we see that my house is gone. Tears spring to my eyes when I remember how beautiful it was and how happy we were there. Now it's gone.

The three of us sit in the cab in the driveway staring at a few scorched timbers sticking up out of the foundation.

Most of the front yard has been burned to the ground, too. The roses, the ornamental trees, the flower beds—they're all gone. The brick wall makes it look even more desolate.

"Is any of the backyard still there?" Zeke asks in a tiny voice.

"Most of the fruit trees are," Danny replies in an undertone. "Most of the fence is gone, though." He clears his throat. "Let's go inside. Staring at it won't bring it back. It will be easier for you to deal with it if you just keep moving."

He gets out and I bend over to pick up my handbag from the floor at my feet. When I sit up, I see Danny coming around to the passenger side to open my door for me. He better not start doing this all the time.

I keep my eyes down while I get out of the truck. I'm not going to make a federal case out of this because I'm not going to stay here for very long. This is just a temporary stopping place until I can figure out a different place for Zeke and me to stay.

Danny helps Zeke out and then Danny picks up all our bags in both hands. He carries everything to the front porch, sets everything down to open the door for us, and then picks everything up again. He doesn't let either of us carry anything.

"Go right on in," he tells us. "Make yourselves at home."

Zeke really does go right on in. He waltzes through the front door like he's been here a million times.

I step across the threshold, but the sight of Danny's living room makes me a thousand times more uncomfortable if that's even possible. This is the spot where we made out. That couch over there.....

That couch will never be a couch to me—not ever again. It will always be the place where Danny and I......

I get a rush of memories, but there's nowhere else to look. The whole living room is that and nothing else.

Zeke goes straight to the fireplace and gazes up at all of Danny's decorations. I really need to nip this in the bud. Zeke's fascination with Danny could become something I don't want to deal with when the time comes for us to move on.

Danny disappears upstairs with our stuff. I hear him moving around up there so I take the opportunity to sit down in the armchair and pull Zeke toward me.

"Listen, sweetie," I tell him. "I know you like Danny and everything and I know you're really happy to be out of the shelter, but you have to remember that we're just guests here. Danny is doing something really nice for us by letting us stay here....."

I have to break off when Danny comes downstairs. He goes into the kitchen and comes out frowning at his phone. "We need to get your head checked out, buddy. There might be something wrong with it if it's still hurting after three days."

He holds the phone to his ear and I hear it ringing. "What are you doing?" I ask.

"I'm calling Ellen about Zeke's head injury."

I freeze and my eyes bug out. "You're calling Ellen—Ellen from the hospital—the paramedic?"

"She's John's wife. She's my sister-in-law. If I can't get hold of her, I could call Leila. She's Keith's wife and she's the fire crew paramedic who took care of Zeke the night of the...." He jumps and his tone changes. "Hey, sweetie. It's me. Yeah, hi. I just brought Zeke and Emily home to my house. They're staying here. Yeah, hey, I wanted to ask you about Zeke's head injury. He says he's still in pain, but it should have resolved by now, shouldn't it, if it was just a concussion like you said?"

He listens for a minute. I can't believe what I'm hearing.

I get a flashback to that night at the hospital. No wonder Ellen was being so affectionate with Danny.

I have to rearrange my whole world, now that I know all the connections between these people.

That woman—the paramedic with the leg brace—she's Chief Brewer's wife—and the paramedic who took care of Zeke the night of the fire.....

I can't imagine Keith being married to anyone, but why not? He's as nice and considerate and helpful as John and Danny. Keith just looks like someone you wouldn't want to meet in a dark alley—or anywhere else for that matter.

I don't really know anything about him, though. I don't know anything about any of the Brewer brothers. They're strangers.

Danny listens to someone talking on the other end of the phone and then he walks over to Zeke. Danny studies Zeke while he listens.

Then Danny says, "No, he sees fine apart from that. No, he's walking around and making eye contact. He's been holding a decent conversation all the way home."

Ellen talks to him a little longer and then he says, "Thanks, sweetheart. I really appreciate it."

He hangs up and turns to Zeke. "She says having bad headaches isn't unusual, but to keep an eye on things. If it gets worse instead of better, we should go back in and get you checked out. In the meantime, she says I can give you some ibuprofen if you need it."

"I'm okay," Zeke tells him. "I feel better now that we're out of the shelter."

"I'm not surprised." Danny heads back to the kitchen and talks over his shoulder on the way. "The alcohol fumes in that place were giving *me* a headache."

He rummages in the fridge and comes back with two glasses of lemonade. He hands one to Zeke and sets one on the coffee table in front of me.

I try to avoid looking at him. Why is he being so nice to me?

He doesn't notice my rudeness when I don't pick up the glass. He's already going into the kitchen and taking more stuff out of the fridge. "Do you want a sandwich, buddy?" he calls.

"Thanks!" Zeke goes over there and climbs onto the bar stool. They keep yammering away to each other like they've known each other all their lives. "When can I see the book, Danny?"

"Which one, pal?"

"The one on how to become a firefighter."

"Oh, that. Here." Danny pulls a booklet from under the phone-book at the end of the kitchen counter. He hands it to Zeke to read while Danny keeps making sandwiches. "Emily—do you want a sand-wich?"

"Um....." I hesitate.

I shouldn't. I don't want to take anything from Danny, but I can't keep throwing his hospitality back in his face.

The glass of lemonade drips dewy drops of water on the coffee table. I really want to drink it and he'll get offended if I don't. He'll probably get offended if I do anything to throw his hospitality back in his face. Why wouldn't he? I really am being rude.

"Um....okay," I finally say, and since I'm accepting a sandwich, I pick up the glass and take a swig of the lemonade, too.

It tastes delicious and instantly makes me feel better. The sting of winding up in a homeless shelter fades—slightly.

"This is so complicated!" Zeke exclaims while he turns the pages. "What does, 'extrication' mean?"

"It means getting a trapped person out of wherever they're trapped," Danny explains. "Say someone got in a car accident and the car got crushed and all the doors were so smashed that you couldn't open them to get the person out. Extrication means you have special procedures for cutting the car open so you can get to the person."

"But you didn't do any special procedures to get me and Mom out of the house. You just went in and got us."

"Yeah, and look at me." Danny holds up his bandaged hands for Zeke to see. "The safety of the crew is paramount. No one is sup-posed to go into a burning building or any other dangerous situation without the right protective gear and safety measures to make sure the rescue crew comes out alive and unhurt. That didn't happen with me—as you can see."

"But we would have died if you didn't come in. What are you supposed to do then?"

"Well, in that situation, I wasn't on the fire crew, was I? I was just some random dude who happened to notice the house next door on fire. If I'd been in another house and not been a firefighter, I would have done the same thing and I still would have gotten hurt. If I had been working on the crew that night, we would have used a ladder to get up to that window and I would have been dressed in full protective turn-outs. We would have used an axe to break that window instead of me doing it with my hand like an idiot."

"You aren't an idiot!" Zeke insists.

Danny smiles at him across the counter. "Thanks, buddy. I would do it all again in a heartbeat. Getting hurt was worth it to make sure you two are okay." He hands a plate across the counter, puts it in front of Zeke, and takes the booklet away. "This is for adults—not kids. You concentrate on your schoolwork. That's the best way you're going to be able to understand this."

Zeke looks down at his plate. "Mom says I shouldn't go back to school as long as Dad's in town."

A chill falls over the room and I feel Danny watching me from across the room. I can't even send my son to school because it's too dangerous.

Danny finally breaks the silence. "I think your mom's right. I don't think you should go to school until the Police figure out whatever they're gonna do about this situation."

"I have to go to school!" Zeke insists. "I can't stay locked up in the house the whole time! That's why we moved here—so we could have a normal life and I could go to school! I've been alone for years—practically my whole life!"

"Easy, buddy," Danny murmurs. "No one is keeping you locked up in the house. Those days are over. I can find some kids for you to play with. You don't have to be alone. It's just that the teachers don't know your situation. If your dad showed up at the school and tried to take you away, the teachers wouldn't be able to stop him. All we want is to keep you safe so you don't have to go through what you went through before."

Zeke looks up. His voice cracks with tormented emotion. I did that. I did that to my own son. "Could you really find some kids for me to play with?"

"Sure. I can do that right now." Danny pulls out of his phone again. He makes a few calls and then hangs up. "John said he can bring Oakleigh over on the weekend, but we have a firehouse barbecue at the beach this weekend anyway. You can come to that. There will be tons of kids there and plenty of adults around to keep an eye on things. Your dad wouldn't dare to try anything there."

Zeke's head shoots up and he gasps in delight. "Really?! I could really do that?!"

"Sure. It will be good for you to get out to the beach and run around with a bunch of other kids. Now finish your sandwich and then you can go play in the backyard if you want to. I gotta do a few things before dinner."

Chapter 11: Emily

I can't sit still from the tension in Danny's house, but I also realize that the tension is completely one-sided. I'm the only one who feels even marginally tense.

Zeke runs in and out through the back door, plays in the backyard, comes back in to talk Danny's ear off about everything, and then goes off to explore the house.

I can't make up my mind whether to stay sitting in the living room or pace around the house.

Zeke sticks his head down the stairs. "My stuff is in a huge room up here!"

"That's where you're staying, buddy!" Danny calls back. "Your mom is down the hall and I'm at the end. If you want to switch, do it now."

Zeke bursts out laughing. "Can I switch with you?"

"No, but you can sleep on the couch if you want to."

Zeke laughs again and runs back outside. I can't keep sitting here, but when I stand up and pace, I come face to face with everything else in this room that I'm already familiar with—Danny's decorations, pictures of him with his family, the back of the couch, the wall by the door.....

I go into the dining room to watch Zeke playing in the backyard. He can go back and forth between Danny's yard and the part of my old yard that's still green and growing. I try not to look at the blackened part of the yard closer to where the house used to be.

Danny keeps messing around in the kitchen. He bangs the pots and pans, and when I glance in there, I see him cutting up vegetables and putting them in a bowl.

He surprises me out of my wits by actually talking to me—as if he would bring me to stay here without trying to talk to me. "We should drive into town over the weekend and buy whatever clothes or gear you and Zeke need. He'll need clothes and school supplies and stuff for whenever he starts back to school....and you'll need clothes and stuff, too."

Danny doesn't look up from his work when he says this. He says it so casually like this is all a normal part of his daily life. Maybe it is. How should I know?

"I don't want to put you to that kind of expense," I tell him. "You're already doing enough for me—for us."

He looks up and makes a face before he goes back to work. "Don't give me that. You wouldn't have taken your injured son to a homeless shelter if you had any money. You need stuff and you aren't going to get it on your own. What did you think—that I would just let you go through life with one change of clothes? Don't insult me."

He keeps saying that and I know he's right. I just hate relying on him—or anyone. I wouldn't feel comfortable accepting this help from a stranger or even someone neutral like Ellen or Chief Brewer.

Danny doing it makes it so much worse, though. I should be able to take care of myself and Zeke better than this.

I stare out the window, but I can't see Zeke anymore. He goes down into the long grass by the fruit trees. I see the grass moving, but I don't watch him. He's as safe here as he's ever going to be.

"I was planning on getting a job when I moved to town," I mumble more to myself than to Danny.

"What did you think you might do?" he asks over his shoulder.

"I don't know. I don't have any training. I met Colin when I was seventeen and he never let me work. I didn't even finish high school."

Danny shakes his head. He's still standing there with his back to me. "He really is a scumbag. The good news is that your life is a blank slate. You can write whatever you want on it. You can let your imagination run wild, come up with your dream job, and go for it. There's nothing stopping you."

"I don't know how to do anything," I insist. "I never even passed the GRE."

"Well, then that's your first step. You're smart enough. You could probably pass it without even studying. Right?"

I shrug and don't look away from the window. I really am my own worst enemy. I think of myself as already defeated, but when he puts it like that, I know he's right. I never had any problem getting good grades in school.

He finishes what he was doing, turns around, and studies me while he leans against the counter. "What's your dream job? What would you do if you could do anything in the world?"

I shrug again. "I don't want to say it out loud. You'll laugh at me."

"Of course I won't laugh at you. Come on. Spill it. What job do you think is so great that you would never be able to do it because it's too great for you?"

I turn bright red and turn back to the window. "I can't say."

"Come on! How bad can it be?"

I glance over at him, and when I see him grinning at me, I can't look away. "I guess.....I don't know.....I think it's pretty great the way all these women paramedics are out there saving everybody. It would be pretty great if I could do what you do—except in more of a medical sense instead of a charge-into-a-burning-building and save-the-day kind of way. I like their style of doing things. The paramedics that worked on you and Zeke were.....well, yeah, that's the kind of job I would say is too great for me."

His jaw drops. "You want to be a paramedic—on the fire crew?"

"I didn't say that, but it would be pretty freakin' awesome. I can't argue with Zeke about that."

Danny shuts his mouth with difficulty and goes back to working in his kitchen. He turns off the oven and takes a pitcher of lemonade out of the fridge. He keeps shaking his head.

"What?" I ask. "I told you you'd laugh at me."

"Did you hear me laugh? I think it's fantastic. You should do it."

"Naw. I couldn't."

He turns around fast. "You see? Right there. You're telling yourself you can't, but there's no reason you couldn't. You don't even need a high school diploma for that."

Now it's my turn to have my jaw hit the floor. "You don't?"

"Of course not. You could take the GRE and go straight into an EMT course. Well, I think you need basic first aid first, but you could take that in a weekend at the firehouse. Then you'd take the EMT course and you'd be in." He snaps his fingers. "Yes! John would be delighted. He can never find enough good EMTs—and don't even get me started on paramedics. You could get a job at the firehouse pretty much as soon as you got your certification."

"Really?" I can't stop staring at him. He's right. This opens up a whole world of possibilities. Then I wilt. "No, I couldn't."

"Why not? What do you have to lose?"

I shut my mouth and turn back to the window. I can't answer him, but I can think of a lot of reasons I couldn't.

For a start, I couldn't put myself in that kind of danger when I have a child to raise. I wouldn't want to work long shifts when Zeke needs me at home.

"I was thinking something more like getting a job as a secretary."

Danny bends over the sink, sticks out his tongue, and makes a puking sound. "Please. You would never be happy doing that."

"Why not? Of course I would. What makes you say I wouldn't?"

He grimaces at me again. "Please. Look who you're talking to. I've been around paramedics and firefighters all my life. I've seen enough people come and go through the firehouse. The minute someone even thinks they might like to do emergency work, it's all downhill from there. If someone dreams or fantasizes about becoming a firefighter, EMT, or paramedic, they won't be happy doing anything else—especially not a desk job." He retches into the sink again. "Ugh! No thank you! I mean, just look at Ellen. She's the proof right there."

"Ellen? What about her?"

"She worked on the fire crew for years. Didn't you know?"

"Of course not. How could I know? I've only seen her at the hospital."

"Well, she worked on the front line for years. She was our best medic on the rescue truck before she got hurt on the job. She went through months of agony trying to get her life back. Losing the truck was the worst thing that ever happened to her, but things got worse when she tried to find another job that would accommodate her disability. She couldn't find anything that made her as happy as the fire crew. Then she found that job at the hospital and it's perfect for her. Once someone starts doing emergency work, they don't go back."

I turn back to the window. That story about Ellen only reinforces in my mind that I could never do anything like that. I might get hurt and then I wouldn't be able to take care of Zeke. I couldn't let that happen.

I admire women like Ellen, Leila, and the other paramedics who took care of Danny and Zeke. Those women have something I don't. I wish I could be as tough and caring and strong as they are, but that's never going to happen. I have too much working against me.

Chapter 12: Emily

D anny slides open the glass doors leading to his back porch and yells across the yard. "Zeke! Come inside for dinner, buddy!"

Zeke comes running. He looks so happy playing outside in the yard because he is happy. I've never been able to give him that, either. I really made a mess of his life and mine.

Danny rumples Zeke's hair when Zeke crashes into the house. "Go wash your hands before dinner, pal," Danny tells him.

"I never had to do that at home," Zeke counters.

"Well, you aren't at home anymore, are you?" Danny tells him. "Go wash your hands. You've been playing out there in the dirt. You wash your hands before you eat. Go!"

He shoves Zeke toward the bathroom. Zeke obeys Danny much better than Zeke has ever obeyed me. I guess that's just another problem with him growing up with an abusive father. Colin never listened to a word I said so Zeke doesn't, either.

Danny sees me standing there and waves to the table. "How about you wash your hands, too?"

I turn bright red, but I take myself off to the bathroom anyway. Fortunately for me, Zeke is already done and racing back to the living room, so he doesn't see me washing my hands after him.

I get to the table just as Zeke is sitting down. Danny pours him a glass of lemonade and then one for me and one for himself. He goes back and forth to the kitchen bringing salad, pasta, and a big dish of green beans smothered in butter.

"This is awesome!" Zeke exclaims. "We never eat like this at home."

"Well, you better get used to it because we eat a lot around here."

"Who's we?" I ask before I think to stop myself.

"All three of us." He goes back to the kitchen and brings a foil-covered baking dish from the oven. The dish looks familiar.

He puts it in the middle of the table.

"What's that?" Zeke asks.

"It's cannelloni. Your mom made it, so I hope you like Italian food." Danny rips off the foil. One three-inch square has been carved out of the corner. Other than that, it's the same casserole I made for him.

Danny doesn't tell Zeke that, though. Danny throws the foil away and sits down. Zeke picks up his fork and his eyes widen when he sees all the food in front of him.

Before any of us can do anything, Danny folds his hands, bows his head, and says, "Bless us, O Lord, in these, Thy gifts, which we are about to receive, and may the Lord make us truly thankful. Amen."

He raises his head, picks up the serving spoon, and starts scooping out a hunk of cannelloni.

Zeke and I sit frozen in our chairs. Are we supposed to do anything? Danny doesn't even notice that neither Zeke nor I joined him in saying that prayer.

I don't know how to react and I catch Zeke shooting me a questioning glance, but Danny doesn't miss a beat. He sticks out his hand to Zeke. "Give me your plate, buddy."

Zeke scrambles to hand over his plate and Danny dumps a massive pile of cannelloni on it. I guess that's the signal. Maybe Danny said that prayer for all of us. He even serves himself another matching hill of pasta and starts eating.

"I have to work tomorrow," he tells me. "so I was thinking we should call Jim Walker and have him assign some of his guys to drive by the house during the day just to make sure our friend doesn't drop by."

I'm still trying to get my brain to function. I bend over the salad and green beans to serve myself and then Zeke. "I guess so."

"It's either that or have him assign a uniformed officer to stand guard out front," Danny goes on. "I don't think we're ready for that. Do you? You know Colin better than I do, but I don't think he'll quit just because you came to stay here."

"No, he won't quit," I mumble.

"What do you say to coming to the firehouse barbecue on Saturday?" he asks.

"Yes!" Zeke chimes in. "We have to go!"

Danny grins at him. "Sometimes we even take tents and camp out overnight. It's a hoot."

"Yes!" Zeke practically yells. "I am so doing that! So who are the other kids? Are they in my class at school?"

"Well, there's Oakleigh, John's and Ellen's daughter. There's Felix and Ainsley, Cameron's and Olivia's kids. I think there are about twelve others. I don't know what classes they're in. You'll just have to meet them and find out."

"I might already know them," he suggests. "I might have already met them at school."

"Yeah, that's right." Danny glances over at me.

I don't say anything about going to the barbecue. I'm not sure I want to have anything to do with people who know my whole disastrous backstory. In fact, I'm certain I don't want to have anything to do with people who know my whole disastrous backstory.

They all know my disastrous present story, too. That's the worst part. If Danny knows about me winding up in a homeless shelter after my psycho husband burned down my house, the whole firehouse probably knows.

That's another reason I could never work there. I couldn't stand having everyone looking at me knowing what a trainwreck my life is.

I pick at my fork. "What's the matter?" Danny teases. "Is the cannelloni no good?"

I wind up blushing and shooting him a grin on the side. "The cook needs to take a few lessons."

"It's fantastic. You can cook here all the time if you want to. You won't hear any argument from me."

"Mom's a great cook," Zeke chimes in.

"The rest of us mere mortals can only hope to learn from her," Danny replies and turns back to me. "Eat up. I know you didn't eat much when you were staying at the shelter."

I look up. "What makes you say that?"

He doesn't answer. He levels me with a direct stare and then shoots a meaningful glance at Zeke.

That look tells me all I need to know. Danny is too observant not to see how hungry Zeke and I both are. I haven't been able to eat since the fire and I couldn't afford to buy much food even for Zeke.

He plows into his food like he really is starving. He's too good a kid to complain about it, but I know he didn't get enough while we were at the shelter. That's three days of hunger I can add to my tally of things I've done to harm my child.

Danny eats a lot, too. He doesn't hold back, but he has a lot more muscle to feed than the rest of us. He goes back to eating and pretends I didn't just ask that question.

Zeke interrogates Danny about everything firehouse for the rest of the meal. Danny answers as directly as possible. He tells Zeke everything he wants to know and doesn't gloss over anything, not even the bad parts about people getting hurt.

"That's just part of the job," Danny tells Zeke. "We do everything we can to reduce the risks, but no one can make it completely safe. It just doesn't work that way."

Their conversation goes on for the rest of the meal, but Danny never shows any sign of getting bored. He holds up his end of the conversation like it interests him as much as anything else they might talk about.

He doesn't try to engage with me, either, and when we all finish eating, he gets up and starts clearing the table. "Hey, buddy," he tells Zeke. "Go over to the bookshelf there, pick out any book that looks interesting, and bring it over to the kitchen counter."

"What for?" Zeke asks.

"I want you to read it to me," Danny tells him.

"But....they're your books. Can't you read them yourself?"

"Of course, smart aleck. I can read them perfectly well. That's why I want *you* to read them to me. I want to find out how well you can read."

"I can read just fine," Zeke tells him. "Ask Mom."

"I'm not asking her. I'm asking you. If you can read just fine, go get a book and read it to me. You aren't going to school, but that doesn't mean you aren't going to get an education. Now go do it."

Zeke goes over to the bookshelf and takes a long time to pick out a book. Danny clears the table and then starts cleaning the kitchen.

I really should go in there and help him, but I just can't bring myself to get that close to him. I would have to tell him to leave the kitchen if I went in there. Being near him....I don't let myself think about it.

Zeke finally comes back with a book and holds it up. "This looks interesting."

"What is it?" Danny asks over his shoulder.

Zeke holds the book up higher. "This."

"I can't see it, genius. What's the title?"

Zeke frowns at the front cover. "It says....*Treasure Island*."

My head shoots up and I spin around. What is a fully grown firefighter doing with a book like *Treasure Island* on his bookshelf?

"Oh, yeah! That's a good one," Danny yells over his shoulder. "Read that one."

Zeke climbs onto one of the barstools, opens the book, and starts reading about Captain Billy Bones at the Admiral Benbow Inn.

He's a good reader, but he stumbles over some of the old-fashioned wording. He has to stop a few times and Danny calls over his shoulder to tell Zeke whatever the word is that Zeke is having trouble with.

Other than that, Danny doesn't interrupt while he runs water into the sink and puts the dishes in the dishwasher.

I'm feeling more and more like a third wheel and I dread the moment when Danny finishes cleaning up. Then I might actually have to deal with him....in this living room.

I go upstairs and find my stuff in one of the bedrooms. It's a very elegant guest room with a big queen bed piled with cushions and pillows. No way could Danny have set this up for me, which means he keeps it like this all the time.

He's nothing like I expected. He keeps his house clean and orderly with nothing out of place.

I find Zeke's things in another guest room set up exactly the same way. It's obviously set up for an adult, but the third bedroom in the same hall is set up for a kid. A dinosaur bedspread covers the single bed with shelves of toys against one wall.

I can't figure out why Danny didn't put Zeke in here, but Zeke has definitely found this place. A bunch of toys lie on the floor where he's been playing with them.

I go back to my room—or rather to the room I'll be staying in. I can't let myself get comfortable here. This is just a stopping place until I can figure out what to do next.

I definitely need to find a job, which means I need an address. I couldn't use the shelter address while I'm staying here, but using this address means I'll be staying here until I get a job.

I don't want to. I don't want to rely on Danny for anything, much less a place to stay, but I don't have enough money even to stay at the shelter, much less get another place.

I hide in my room until eight o'clock. When I get back to the living room, Zeke is reading the part of the story where blind Pew goes after Jim Hawkins and tries to kill him. Danny sits on the couch listening to Zeke read.

I wait for Zeke to get to the end of his sentence before I interrupt. "Okay, it's time to put the book away for tonight, sweetheart. It's time for you to go upstairs, put away the toys you were playing with, and get ready for bed."

"Aw, Mom!" he howls. "We were just getting to the good part."

"You can read it again tomorrow. You aren't going to bed without cleaning up your mess."

He moans and groans a lot, but he goes upstairs anyway. That leaves me downstairs with Danny. I can't face that, so I go upstairs, too.

I supervise Zeke cleaning up, but he doesn't have any pajamas or a toothbrush.

I'm just about to tell him to go to bed without either when Danny shows up, goes into the room with the toys, and opens the dresser drawer. "There are some pajamas in here you can borrow....and I have some extra toothbrushes under the sink."

He pulls out a pair of white pajamas covered with pictures of dinosaurs. "You said you didn't have any kids," Zeke tells him.

Danny grins. "Oakleigh and some of the other kids stay over here a lot. It pays to be prepared for anything." He shoves the pajamas at Zeke. "Get changed and I'll find you a toothbrush."

Zeke beats it out of the room and Danny's cheeks color when he sees me watching him. "Sorry I don't have a pair for you."

The blood rushes to my face. "I would be worried if you did."

He laughs. "I do have a toothbrush for you." He goes into the bathroom, digs under the sink, and comes out with an unopened package with four toothbrushes in it. He tears open the package and hands me one of the brushes. "Here you go. Make sure you brush in circles away from the gums."

Now it's my turn to laugh. "Yes, Mother."

He goes through the upstairs taking care of every little detail, but he disappears back downstairs when it comes time to put Zeke to bed.

I take him into the other room—the one with the huge queen-sized bed. I tuck him in and then sit down on the mattress next to him.

He sighs with a big smile on his face. "It feels good here, Mom."

"Yeah, it does," I murmur.

"Danny's so nice," Zeke exclaims. "I wish we could stay here all the time."

"Well, at some point, we will have to get our own place. You know that, right?"

A cloud crosses his face. "Then we won't be living next door to Danny anymore. I don't want to live anywhere else."

"I had insurance on the house next door, but it will take a while to rebuild it. It could be months, which means we would need to find another place to live."

"Why can't we just stay here?" he asks. "Danny won't mind."

I lower my eyes and pretend to straighten out of a wrinkle on his pajamas. "I'm sure he wouldn't, but right now, you need to go to sleep. We'll deal with that later."

I kiss him and turn off the light, shut the door, and go back to my own guest room. That's what this is. It's a guest room. I'm not staying here.

Chapter 13: Emily

I sit down on the guest room bed, but I can't settle in. I really need something to do. I can't just keep lingering in this half-space between one thing and another. Whatever I'm going to do, I need to start doing it.

That's why my life is such a mess. I'm between things. I'm between places to live. I'm between Colin and whatever else my life is going to be after Colin. I'm between being an unemployed single mother and being employed.....somewhere.

Danny stays downstairs while I hide upstairs. I really am pathetic for hiding from him, but being in the same room with him would be too much. It might lead to......whatever it might lead to.

I'm still sitting there eating myself up inside when he comes upstairs at nine o'clock. He passes my room without looking and keeps going to the master bedroom at the end of the hall. I hear him moving around in there, but he doesn't shut the door.

I squirm in my seat. Is he going to come in here and try to start something with me? He doesn't come.

I should just shut my door and go to bed. Shutting the door would send him a message that I don't want him to come.

I do want him to come. That's the problem. I keep telling myself I don't when I do. He isn't going to just ignore me, is he?

I told him to leave me alone at the hospital. Does he really plan to just drop it? Did he really bring me and Zeke here just to help us?

I wait another fifteen minutes. I hear his phone beeping in his bedroom, but that's all. Is he really just going to go to sleep....and do nothing?

Insatiable curiosity gets the better of me. I stand up and tiptoe to the guest room door. I can't see him and he can't see me, but my heart pounds that I'm even doing that much.

I really shouldn't go out there. I shouldn't make him think I'm interested when I'm not.

I don't know what's getting into me, but I can't turn back now. If he doesn't do anything—does that mean *he* isn't interested? Did I actually succeed in pushing him away? I can't stand even thinking that.

I take a step out into the hall and glance toward his room. He sits on the end of the bed wearing a pair of loose, dark plaid pajama pants and nothing else. His bare toes dig into the carpet.

The light from a bedside lamp shines on his chiseled shoulders, neck, and chest. He's fiddling around with his phone. He doesn't see me

.

His other hand rests on his thigh in a loose fist. Taking off his shirt has messed up his hair and it falls over his face.

Right then, he stands up, walks over to the nightstand, and turns his back to me to put the phone down on it. Now I can see the huge white bandage taped to his back. It looks even worse like this, now that I know he got hurt saving me and Zeke.

I take one more step closer to his room. If I go in there, it's all over. I won't be able to tell myself that I don't want this because I do. I won't be able to stop it because I don't want to stop it.

I want him. I want the man who got hurt saving me and Zeke—not just once but multiple times. He's by far the kindest, nicest, most caring man I've ever met.

He's also the hottest and the most attractive. He's the man I've been most attracted to in my life. As soon as I think that, all the desire from that first night comes back with a vengeance. I can't walk away from Danny without feeling that again—all of it.

As soon as I think that, he turns around and sees me standing there. I take the last step to his bedroom door and then step inside it. I'm in his bedroom and he's half-naked.

The instant he sees me, I know he wants it, too. He's too considerate to initiate after I told him to leave me alone. He would walk away entirely. That's just the way he's made.

He wants it, though, and the moment he lays eyes on me, he starts getting hard inside his pajamas.

I step closer and he comes to meet me. His eyes burn into mine from directly above, and like something out of a distant dream, he slips his arm behind my back and pulls me against him the way he did in the living room that night.

His hand flattens on the lower curve of my back and he pushes his crotch into me so I can feel how pulsing hard he is. His pajamas leave nothing to the imagination and that hardness lights me up as never before.

He feels incredible and strong and masculine. He doesn't try to hide it from me. He pushes it between my legs and makes me explode with desire for him.

He stares down into my eyes just so he knows and I know that we really are doing this. We both want it. Why deny it?

My flesh aches and quivers to feel just how hard he can get. I want him like never before. I want all of him. I want everything with no holding back.

He stands there smoldering with buried intensity while we both look deeply into each other's eyes. Neither of us can hide in that gaze and I don't want to. I want him to know how much I need this. I want him to know I won't hold back, either. I would never and could never hold back with him.

He bends down and kisses me, and as soon as he starts, the dam breaks. I throw myself into kissing him back and I can't keep my hands off him.

I touch his arms and slide up his chest to his neck and hair. He smells intoxicating and his tongue feels like he's licking me right now.

His hands materialize all over me. They don't feel right with the bandages in the way, but I don't care.

He seizes my ass in a crushing grip, grinds me on his hard package, and then grabs my breast through my shirt. He pulverizes me hard enough to make me moan into his mouth. I can't stop riding his crotch as he digs it into my swollen, flaming tissues.

He mauls my mouth and then dives the same hand between my legs to squeeze me there, too. I squeal in aching desire.

As soon as the frenzy starts, he backsteps to the bed, sits down on the mattress where he was before, and steers my thighs down on either side of his lap.

Now I can ride him as hard as I want. Being in that position with my legs spread turns me on beyond belief.

He grabs my ass again and pumps me down on top of him. His fingers crawl to the back of my jeans and he teases me through the thick denim. I want him to touch me, but we're both attacking each other too hard and too fast to stop.

I wrap my body around him and grind on his pelvis in an unbroken rhythm. I have to feel him. I have to get him inside me before I go insane.

I feel myself spiraling into another climax, but before I can get there, he tips over backward with me attached to him from above.

He doesn't let go of my mouth while his hands range all over my body. He grabs me between the legs and doesn't let go. He rubs and massages and squeezes until I whine and whimper in his mouth. I'm going to lose it soon if he doesn't stop.

I can't ride him like this, but I still need to feel his hardness, so I thrust my hand down inside his pajama pants. He yelps when I grab his hard rod and feel all his veins straining with hot blood.

I stroke him and then dive down further to grab his balls. He gasps and then groans in ecstasy when I touch him. I love that sound.

I tear away from his mouth and bury my face in his crotch. I push his pants out of the way and he collapses whining in agony when I take him in my mouth.

I love hearing how much he needs this. How long has it been for him? Probably not long if he's in the habit of hitting on the nurses at the hospital.

I don't care. If this is a one-time thing, I'm going to enjoy it to the limit. I take him deep into my throat and his hand appears on the back of my neck to guide me.

His breath strains and he fights for air. "Oh, God, baby!" he husks. "Oh, my God!"

I can't stop sucking him. I love how powerful he feels in my mouth and he spasms every time I sink down on him.

Without warning, he attacks me, grabs me by the shoulders, and flips me onto my back on the bed. He pounces on me, and before I can move, he seizes two handfuls of my shirt and strips it open.

I lie before him in nothing but my bra and he plunges between my cleavage. He bites me through my bra cups and then pulls them down.

Now it's my turn to gasp and groan as he sinks his teeth into my nipples and sucks them deeper and harder into his mouth.

Just when I think I can't take any more, he rears up, takes hold of my jeans, and yanks them down as far as my hips. He can't get them any farther than that, not without me lifting my weight off them.

He steers them down and pulls my panties with them. As soon as he drags them off my feet, he dives between my legs, pries my thighs apart, and makes me writhe and thrash on the bed. He attacks me even more ferociously than he did that first night.

I can't stop whimpering and moaning. I hear myself getting louder. I should stop now before Zeke hears.

Danny reads my mind and gets off the bed just long enough to shut the door. Then he storms over to me and falls face first between my thighs again.

I buckle onto the bed sobbing in relief as he buries his tongue in me. He can't use his fingers with the bandages on. I wish he could. I ache for him to pump me full of his fingers and make me climax the way he did before.

He growls to himself while he feasts himself on my flesh. I buck into his face as wave upon wave of desire and pleasure sweep me away. I can't get enough of everything he does to me.

Just when I feel like I'm about to explode, he pushes up onto his hands and knees and crawls up to my mouth. His tongue snakes into my mouth and he suffocates me in a thousand kisses.

I claw at his body. I want him so damn bad. I push down his pajama pants and his eyes pop wide open to stare at me. He won't stop staring into my eyes while we kiss and my hand closes around his shaft. Yes. I want that. I need it. I don't want to wait any longer.

He keeps staring at me in something like disbelief when I use my foot to push his pajama pants the rest of the way down. I spread my legs as wide as they'll go and guide him into the saturated flesh waiting for him.

He clamps his eyes shut and gasps when I pull him all the way in. God damn, he feels good!

He holds himself up on his arms, and as soon as he gets in, he starts pumping for the stars. He makes me yelp every time his thickness blasts me apart, but I meet each thrust with an answering beat upward to take him all the way in. Oh, hell yes. I can't get enough of him.

He flexes his washboard abs to slam all the way to the hilt. Every deep resounding bump knocks me up the bed and my body and breasts bounce where he can see them.

He doesn't stop kissing me and his eyes never let me look away. He sees how much I yearn for him. He sees how hot he makes me. He drives everything else out of my mind until nothing remains but him.

I slid my hands down his back and feel the bandage there, but I stay away from it. I grab his ass and pull him in hard with each stroke. He gasps through his nose as the power builds to an explosive climax.

I arch my back into his thrusts to encourage him. Every stroke makes me yelp and I hear myself starting to scream. At the last second, he tears off my mouth, collapses on top of me, and presses his bared teeth to my ear so I can hear every broken roar of epic release.

He crushes me in his arms as he smashes the rest of the way in. That extra blow of pressure skyrockets me into the stratosphere and I erupt all over him as a jet of hot lava shoots into me.

My muscles lock around him and I feel him pulsing and spasming inside me as our bodies detonate in unstoppable waves of bliss.

Chapter 14: Danny

I topple off Emily and collapse on my bed still shaking from the power of what we just did. My heart won't stop pounding and the tremors rock me up and down my body. My muscles won't stop convulsing as the last waves die away.

I shut my eyes fighting to breathe. Holy Christ, she feels mind-blowing. I want to keep going, but I don't know if I can. She might have milked the last drop of my strength with that one.

Before I can think about even opening my eyes, I feel her moving in bed. She probably wants to go back to the guest room in case Zeke hears us.

Instead, she lies down across me and I feel that she's naked now. She's taken off her bra and shirt that she still had on while we did it.

She writhes on top of me rubbing her breasts, stomach, and magnificent thighs all over me. She rubs her dripping flesh up and down my shaft even though I'm starting to go soft now.

She crawls up to my mouth to kiss me, but only for a second. She migrates down to my neck, nibbles my ears, and then she runs her lips and tongue all over my chest and stomach. She even kisses my arms.

I groan with pleasure. She feels silky and voluptuous, but I'm too exhausted to move. I can only lie here and let her enjoy herself on me.

My mind buzzes with pleasure. I love what she's doing to me even if we aren't actually going at it again.

She won't stop, and when she straddles me and rubs her velvety tissues up and down my shaft again, I feel myself starting to get hard. Everything she does turns me on.

She keeps up that rhythm while she drags her breasts over my chest and stomach. She burrows up to my ear under my hair and her hot breath sears my brain. Oh, my God, she's doing it again.

I gasp in agony, but she's already sliding down on top of me. In seconds, she goes to town slamming herself down on me so much harder than before. I tighten my stomach, all my exhaustion gone.

She snatches a bite from my lips and then drives herself down on me with unbelievable force. The sound of her slamming into me echoes through the room. Will Zeke hear us? She doesn't seem to care.

Without warning, she sits up, props her hands on my chest, and stares down at me while she rides me. Her breasts sway in perfect rhythm and her haunted eyes intoxicate me.

I touch her all over, but she's in her own world right now. Her eyes narrow. She looks witchy and dangerous in her craven desire for me. She digs her fingernails into my chest and pumps her hips harder and faster.

Her soft, plush flesh beats around my shaft. She's driving me to the stars too fast. I can't stop her.

I try to grab onto her to slow her down and control her rhythm, but she's already so far beyond control that she doesn't stop.

She throws back her head and moans. The light glistens on her breasts and hair and skin. She captivates me in the madness of her unbridled passion.

She runs her hand up to my face and that movement of her arms pushes her breasts together. They stick out toward me and invite me to play with them. I pinch and twist and tease them, but that only drives her even farther out of her mind.

Her hips widen to her thighs surrounding my body. I want to preserve her like this. I never want to forget what she looks like right now taking her pleasure from me.

She gallops faster and faster. I try to tell her to stop, but I'm escalating too fast. All at once, her sounds spike a register. Her moans turn to shrill screams and she pounds down on me with brutal force.

I can't take it anymore. She looks so beautiful and mesmerizing like this. I explode inside her, but she doesn't stop rocking. Her juices gush around me, but the torrent doesn't stop flowing back and forth between us.

Pulse after pulse fires from her to me and back to her. I bellow in ecstasy. The sheer power of this climax feels almost painful.

I can barely hold it together by the time she collapses on top of me, but she still doesn't stop. She rubs her body all over me, kisses and licks and sucks and bites every inch of my chest and neck and ears that she can reach, and her hair spills all over me.

I sink into the bed groaning in aching pleasure. She wears me out. I'm the one who's supposed to wear her out, not the other way around.

I try to touch her, but my body turns to goo. I can barely breathe.

She inches up my neck to my face and starts kissing me again. She still straddles me, but I'm too spent to do anything else.

Her mouth consumes me and the taste of her lulls me into a dream trance. I could pass out right here, but she doesn't let me.

She breaks away from my mouth, crawls her lips and tongue back down my body, and her hot, hungry, ravenous mouth clamps on me again.

I whimper in agony. She is not doing this to me. She is not sucking me to make me hard again.

Oh, yes, she is, and man—can she suck! She doesn't let up, not even when I touch her head. She increases the suction and my body responds automatically. Did I say I wanted to do it with her all night long? Be careful what you wish for.

She sucks harder and harder—and I get harder and harder. I get so hard that I need to go again, but she still doesn't stop. Is she going to finish me off like this?

I don't want her to. I want to show her who's boss, because if we keep going like this, I'm going to have to admit that she is. That would never work.

She plays with my balls and digs her fingers into my thighs while she lashes her tongue around my veins. Damn, I need her! I need her so bad.

I can't figure out how to do it to her, though. I need to do it in a way that shows her I'm not finished yet.

That thought rockets me off the bed. This one is all mine. The last one was hers. Now it's my turn.

I push her back onto the bed. She squirms watching me crawl on top of her. She spreads her thighs to take me in again, but we aren't playing that game. We did that once before. Now she's mine.

I flip her onto her stomach and drive into her ass from behind. She sobs in torment. Oh, yeah, baby. You know how this goes.

She tries to kiss me. I use my mouth to push her the rest of the way over and dive into her neck. I bite her under her hair and she squeals from the pain. That sound only propels me over the edge.

I use my knees to push her up onto all fours and then I have her. I arch over her and deliver one penetrating smack after another. I know now that she likes it hard and I give her every inch that she wants.

She gasps and then starts panting as I thrust in deep and true. She backs down on me each time and her inner muscles give a little clench of pleasure every time I tap her ass.

Her wetness spanks against my skin and she throws herself into this with all her animal desire. Something unstoppable takes hold of me and I grab her by the hair to pull her in even harder.

She responds by arching her back and flinging herself against me just as hard. She matches my intensity. I never have to worry about her wanting as much as I can give her.

I don't want it like that, though. I let go of her hair and topple forward. She keeps her thighs apart and propped up on her knees when I throw my weight over her to drive in from behind.

She yelps when I bite her neck and her gasping panting breath answers me when I snarl in her ear. I want her to know I'll never stop taking her like this. I'll never stop owning her and conquering her and making her mine—not until there's nothing left of either of us to keep living.

Chapter 15: Danny

I wake up to the feeling of Emily's mouth sliding down on me. I was sound asleep until right now, but she doesn't attack me in ravenous fury the way she did last night.

She slithers her hot, wet tongue around my shaft even though I'm totally soft and sound asleep. She nibbles me and licks me and then she burrows down and sucks my balls for a while before she comes back up to licking my shaft.

She wakes me up slowly as pleasure floods me. I drift out of my dreamworld and wake up into another one where her mouth envelops me in bliss.

I relax into the pillows and let her do what she wants. She teases me until I start to get hard, but she doesn't drive me to the stars. She just stays down there sucking, licking, nibbling, and sighing in pleasure while she fills me with all this delicious rapture.

I can't even bring myself to touch her or guide her or even to run my fingers through her hair. I just want to lie here and feel this. I never want it to stop.

She strokes her hands up my chest, touches my neck and face, and then grasps my thighs and stomach to stabilize herself. Everything she does tells me she's enjoying this as much as I am.

The longer this goes on, the harder I get until my shaft throbs for release. I want to grab her hair and shove her down....but at the same time, I don't want to do that.

I try to sit up, and before I know what she's doing, she grabs me and pulls me over on top of her without letting go of me with her mouth.

The next thing I know, I'm on top of her balls deep in her mouth. She doesn't stop. She just adjusts her position so I thrust right down into her throat.

That position blasts me apart and I explode right into her mouth before I can stop myself. I gasp and moan in aching release. I don't want it to end like this. I would rather have done it with her for real.

She strokes my chest and stomach from underneath, and when I start to blow, she grabs my ass and crams me all the way down into her mouth. She swallows everything and gives the most satisfied moan of pleasure that I've ever heard.

I collapse off her shaking with the tension. I have to go to work this morning. I don't have time to do it with her any other way.

I'll just have to make up for it tonight. That's all there is to it.

She climbs on top of me and starts kissing me even before I can summon the energy to open my eyes. "Don't you have to work this morning?" she mumbles between kisses.

"Are you trying to trap me and keep me locked in the house?" I mutter back.

She chuckles, climbs off me, and lies down next to me a few inches away so she's sure not to touch me. "There. Does that make it easier?"

I throw myself on top of her, pin her, and sink my teeth into her neck. "No, but this does."

She squeals again and then starts moaning when I kiss under her ear.

"You better be quiet or you'll wake up Zeke," I tell her.

She quiets down a little, but just then, she claws at me again and accidentally touches the bandage on my back.

I roar in pain and she springs away—as well as she can considering I'm lying on top of her. "Aargh!" I bellow. "Aaargh!!"

"I'm so sorry!" she exclaims. "I'm so sorry! I didn't mean to!"

"It isn't your fault!" I roll away, but I can't stop snarling in agony. I didn't feel this when I was lying on the bandage last night. It's only the direct pressure of her touch that set me off.

I sit up on the edge of the bed gasping and sweating until the pain fades, but it doesn't go away completely.

Emily sits up next to me and touches the part of my shoulder that isn't covered by a bandage. "I'm so sorry! I really didn't mean to."

"I know that!" I snap more harshly than I mean to. "It isn't your fault."

I hang my head and shut my eyes. Damn, that hurt!

"Can I do anything?" she asks in a small voice.

"You already did." I kiss her and stand up. She's right. I have to get moving so I get to work on time. "Thank you for last night. It was amazing."

She blushes and starts picking up her clothes. "I better go back to my room so I can pretend I've been there all along."

I go get in the shower. When I come out, she isn't in my room anymore.

I don't want to make the bed. I want to leave it like this as a monument to the night I spent with her. I want every night to be like last night.

If every night is like last night, then every morning will have to be like this morning—which means me going to work.

I get dressed and comb my hair. When I get out of the bedroom, I hear Zeke and Emily talking downstairs. I also hear pots and pans banging around down there.

When I show up in the dining room, she's already setting the table for three for breakfast. She blushes at me when she puts a cup of coffee next to my plate. "I didn't know how you like it, so here's the milk and sugar."

"Thank you." I sit down just as Zeke shows up still wearing his pajamas. He yawns and sits down across from me still rubbing the sleep out of his eyes.

Before I can say a word, she puts a plate in front of me piled with scrambled eggs, bacon, and buttered toast. I don't know what to say. *Thank you,* doesn't really cut it.

Zeke doesn't seem to notice the implications of her making me breakfast—but why would he? He's a seven-year-old kid.

She serves him a much smaller breakfast of just eggs and toast and then she sits down at the table to eat with us. She catches me watching her, colors, and bends over her plate.

"Your reading was really good last night, buddy," I tell Zeke. "I can tell you're gonna do great in school."

"He's always been good at reading. It's one of the few things we actually were allowed to do."

"We never read *Treasure Island*, though," he mumbles. He's still half asleep.

"That sucks," I tell him. "It's a really good book. It should be part of every kid's childhood."

"Was it a part of yours?" he asks.

"Absolutely. John started reading it to us."

"Who's us?" he asks.

"Me and Keith. John read it first and he told us we had to hear it, so he started reading it to us. Then it just kind of took over our lives and we started playing pirates all the time."

He stares at me across the table. "For real?"

"Sure. We had a fort in the backyard where we'd act out the part of the book where Jim and the……"

I freeze with the words on my lips when I realize. He hasn't read the book.

He doesn't know anything beyond where Pew tries to kill Jim. Zeke doesn't know about the pirates or the stockade or any of the battles or anything. I don't want to ruin it for him.

He sees my hesitation and lowers his eyes to his plate. "I hate being an only child. You're lucky you have two brothers."

"All the more reason why you should come to the barbecue and meet some more kids." I turn to Emily. "What are you doing today?"

Zeke interrupts. "Mom, can I go outside?"

"Sure, sweetie. Just put your clothes on first."

He races off upstairs. I take the opportunity to ask again. "What are you going to do today?"

She shrugs over her breakfast. "I don't know. I think I might check the real estate listings and see if I can find us a place to live."

I stare at her as the penny drops. "You….you want to move out?"

"Isn't that what this is all about? We're just staying here until we can find somewhere else. I'm sure you didn't mean for us to move in long-term."

"I didn't at first, but now I want you to."

Her head shoots up. "What?"

"Move in. I mean, stay here—permanently. I want you to."

She looks away, but she doesn't eat. She just pushes her eggs back and forth on the plate. "I don't think that's a good idea."

"It's a great idea! You're already here and we're already involved....."

"We are not involved." She shoots out of her chair, snatches her plate, and takes off back to the kitchen.

I'm on my feet in an instant and I follow her in there. "What's the matter? This is perfect. What could be better than this? You know this is what's best for Zeke and for you. Hell, it's what's best for me! Why are you running away from this?"

"This is not what's best for us and it definitely isn't what's best for you." She puts her dish in the sink still loaded with food. Then she goes back for Zeke's plate.

I follow her all the way, but I can't keep arguing with her when Zeke comes downstairs. He only stays for a second before he charges away into the backyard and vanishes under the fruit trees again.

"What's the problem?" I ask once he's gone. "Last night was great. Wasn't it? Don't tell me you didn't enjoy it."

"Oh, I enjoyed it. You know I did. I enjoyed it a little too much."

"How is that possible? It could be like this all the time. Come on. I want you here—both of you."

She snorts at me and turns her back on me. "Stop it."

"What?!" I demand. "Is there a problem between me and Zeke that I don't know about?"

"Stop it, Danny," she snaps. "You know he worships the ground you walk on. That doesn't mean we're moving in here and it doesn't mean you and I are involved. Us having a good time last night doesn't mean anything."

My blood runs cold at those words. "Is that all it was to you? I don't believe you."

She sighs with her back to me. She faces the kitchen sink, but she doesn't do anything. She just stands there bowed and devastated. I've never met anyone as crushed by circumstances.

"Listen," she murmurs. "I really appreciate what you're doing, but it just won't work."

I can't stop staring at the back of her head. She did not just call last night a good time. Hell no.

I want to rage at her and demand that she take that back. She better not have meant it in the way I think she meant it. She better not mean that she used me as a good time so she could feel better about herself. I won't stand that.

I take a step back while I pull myself together. I have to think. I have to deal with this rationally.

One other thing I know for certain. I have to settle this now before I leave for the day. I can't walk out that door with this hanging over our heads.

"Turn around," I tell her in as calm a tone as I can. "Whatever you have to say to me, you turn around and say it to my face."

She turns around, but it takes her at least fifteen seconds before she summons the courage to look me in the eye.

"Now tell me why you think it won't work," I tell her.

She takes another shaky breath. "Look. I understand what you're saying and it *would* be the best thing for me and Zeke, but it wouldn't be the best thing for you. You know that. You.....you deserve better."

"Why do you say that? Why do you think it wouldn't be the best thing for me? I think I know what's best for me."

"Oh, come on. You don't want to get with a single mother whose life is in the gutter."

"Why not? What part of this do you think I don't want? I just told you I do."

She stares at me and then snorts again. "Because I have a kid, Danny. I have a kid who isn't yours and whose father wants to steal him back just as soon as Colin can get his hands on Zeke."

"I know that. I know all of that. So what are you telling me that I don't already know?"

She stares at me even harder and then throws up her hands. She gets busy clearing the table while she talks to me over her shoulder. "You need someone you can build a life with. You need someone you can start a family with and take to your barbecues and all that. That isn't m e."

"You think getting together with you would be bad for me because you have a kid," I repeat. "Is that the only reason?"

"Apart from what a disaster my life is? Yeah."

I don't say anything for a minute. I stand there watching her walk back and forth between the table and the sink. She packages up all the leftover food and puts it in the fridge before she starts doing the dishes.

I take a long time to decide what to say. I don't want to accept what she's telling me, but insisting that she do it my way sure isn't helping.

I finally make up my mind and lean back against the opposite counter. "I've only had one relationship," I tell her.

She spins around fast. "What?"

"I've only been with one other woman and she was a single mother. She had two kids—a boy and a girl. They were five and four when I met them and we lived together for three years. I thought it was forever and I wanted to raise the kids as my own. I bought this house so we could live together and be a family."

She gapes at me with huge eyes. She hardly breathes.

I have to take another deep breath to say the rest of it. "Then I found out she was still married. Her husband showed up one day, made her a bunch of promises, and she left me and took the kids to go back with him. I was just as wrecked over losing the kids as I was over losing her. I could have let her go, but not the kids."

She turns away from me immediately. "Well, I'm still married, too, so that's another reason."

"Would you ever go back to him?"

She whips around just as fast. "God, no! How can you even ask that? Of course I wouldn't! He tried to kill me—and he tried to kill Zeke in that fire. I would never go back to him."

"Then what exactly is your argument against us getting together? I love Zeke. I would love to help you raise him. Come on, Emily. You know this is right. So your life is a mess right now, but it won't always be. I can help you get through it and then we'll be stronger afterward. We can be a family."

"No," she growls over her shoulder. "You think you can protect me from Colin, but you can't. I don't want to inflict my problems on you. You've already gotten hurt in this disaster. I don't want it to get any worse."

I ease up behind her and murmur in her ear from behind. "Maybe I want your problems. Did you ever think of that?"

"Well, you can't have them." She bursts away and strides across the room heading for the stairs. "It's bad enough that I have them. They're mine to deal with and that's the way it's going to stay."

Chapter 16: Emily

I spend an hour watching Zeke playing in the backyard before I dare to come downstairs. I wait until I hear the front door shut and Danny's truck drive away before I set foot out of the guest room.

I really am a spineless coward for hiding from him, but no way can I get involved with him.

That story he told about his former relationship does something to me. He really wants this. He actually said he loves Zeke and I know it's true. It's written all over both of them.

Why can't I accept that? I just don't want something else to go wrong—something that might hurt Danny even more than he's already been hurt.

Ellen said he's going to carry that scar for life because Colin tried to kill me and Zeke. Danny is walking around with his hands, feet, and back bandaged right now because I brought my problems into his life.

I finish cleaning the kitchen, and when I go back to the sliding glass door to check on Zeke, I see him talking to someone next door. They're in my old backyard. No one should be over there.

My hackles rise when I see that the person is a man. Colin better not have sent some other lowlife to mess with Zeke.

I storm out through the sliding glass doors and cross the yard. I get halfway there before the guy notices me, turns around, and I see that it's Fire Chief Brewer—Danny's brother, John.

He smiles at me and then tries to hide it when he sees my expression. "How are you doing?" he asks me. "Zeke was just telling me about you two coming to stay with Danny."

"What are you doing here?" I ask and realize too late that I sound like I'm challenging him. "No one is supposed to be on the property without a warrant from the Police Department."

He holds up a clipboard. I can't read the writing from here. "I'm just finishing the arson workup for the crime lab. Maybe you could help me out. Your bedroom was over there, wasn't it?" He points to the east side of the foundation.

I nod. I don't want to let my guard down, but I have to admit he has a legitimate reason to be on the property. I just don't want him talking to Zeke—God knows why.

I have nothing against Chief Brewer—or any of the rest of the fire crew for that matter. Why should I? They've been great to me and Zeke since day one.

Chief Brewer scowls at his clipboard and jots down a few things. "The octane readings were the highest on that side of the house, so that confirms your statements and Danny's and all the other witness statements. The blood chemical analysis on Zeke and Danny also confirm that they had octane vapors in their lungs, which proves that....."

"Hold it!" I snap. "What blood chemical analysis? I never heard about this."

"The hospital did blood chemical screens on both of them. They didn't do one on you because you weren't technically a patient."

"But I never gave consent for any blood chemical analysis on Zeke. I should have heard about this."

"Actually, there's a clause in the city emergency management charter that states that anyone who calls 911 or who becomes an emergency medical or fire operations patient is giving implied consent for rescue and medical personnel to provide any and all treatment necessary to preserve life and limb. Zeke was semi-conscious if not outright unconscious when he got to the hospital. The medical staff had to determine what was causing his altered state. It could have been a life-threatening brain injury or it could have been a toxic dose of some chemical—an inhaled chemical, in this case. They would have had to treat him with certain drugs to detoxify his blood. Either way, they found levels of octane in his blood and in his lung tissue that could have caused him to pass out. So you can see that they didn't have a choice about it. It was a life-threatening emergency, so they were empowered to take the blood screen without getting specific consent from you for every single procedure."

I shift my weight to my other foot. He really knows his stuff. I can't fault him for that. He knows so much more about this than I do. I feel inferior by comparison.

Zeke cocks his head to one side and studies Chief Brewer intently. Zeke listens to every word out of Chief Brewer's mouth—of course. Chief Brewer is a natural authority. Everyone obeys him. It just comes naturally to him to be in charge.

He doesn't even think he did anything special by telling me all that. He consults his clipboard. "Anyway, the octane vapors would have to be off the charts inside the house to saturate their bloodstreams that much—which means the perp used a lot of octane to start the fire. I'd say he'd get at least two counts of attempted murder for that—plus any other crimes the investigation can pin on him."

I open my mouth to answer, but no sound comes out. Colin is turning out to be even more pathologically insane than even I realized.

Chief Brewer waits for me to say something else. When I don't, he glances down and sees Zeke staring up at him in rapt fascination.

Chief Brewer grins at him. "Hey, you two should come to the next firehouse barbecue. It's tomorrow at the beach….."

"No," I snap a lot louder than I mean to. "We aren't doing that."

He startles at my response. "Why not? Danny can…."

"Danny and I aren't involved. I don't know what he told you…."

He raises his eyebrows. "I didn't think you were. It's none of my business either way. Danny is a big boy. He can choose a good woman for himself."

I have to look away. "We aren't going to the barbecue."

"I didn't mean you could come as his date or anything. I only meant you could come because you're new in the neighborhood. Zeke will be going to school with all our kids. He could meet them if he hasn't already and he could play with them if he has met them. It would be good for both of you to meet a bunch of local people and hang out in a no-pressure environment. That's all I meant."

I pull my head down between my shoulders and don't say anything. If I was ever even slightly tempted to go to the barbecue, I'm not now. This conversation cured me of that.

Chief Brewer turns away. "I'm done here, so I'll see you two around. It's up to you if you want to come to the barbecue. The invitation is there if you change your mind."

He heads back to the foundation and keeps going through the gate in the brick wall. A second later, his red Fire Department pickup drives off down the block.

"Mom!" Zeke hisses. "How could you talk to him like that? He's the fire chief!"

"I know who he is, sweetheart. Come back over to Danny's yard. I don't want you playing over here."

I try to take his hand, but he yanks it out of my grasp. "We *are* going to the barbecue! I don't care what you say! I've been locked up in a house my whole life! I'm going to the barbecue and I'm going to play with the other kids and YOU CAN'T STOP ME!!"

"Sweetheart....!"

"I'M GOING!!" he shrieks and sprints off across the yard to Danny's house. Zeke rushes through the sliding door and doesn't shut it behind him. I hear his footsteps running upstairs.

I don't care what he says, either. We are NOT going to that barbecue. No way. I have enough problems with Danny Brewer. He already thinks we're together. Going to the barbecue would only make it w orse.

Chapter 17:
Danny

I pull my truck into the driveway and instantly get a wonderful feeling when I remember. I'm not coming home to an empty house anymore. Zeke and Emily are here.

I can't wait to see both of them. This is right. I know it is. I just have to convince Emily. The question is how to do that.

I make up my mind while I take my duffel bag out of the back. I won't do or say anything to her about it. I'll just leave it alone and let it grow on her organically. Forcing the issue will only drive her away.

I hate to think how this will affect Zeke. I don't know how he feels about his dad. I should probably find out.

I don't want him to think I'm trying to replace his father. Zeke might really love his father. The kid would resent me for trying to take that away from him.

I walk into the house, and before I can even shut the door, Emily rushes me and gets in my face. "What did you tell John about us?"

"Huh?" I ask.

"Your brother John!" Her voice rises into the nose-bleed range. "I'm sure you know who I'm talking about! What did you tell him about us?"

"Nothing. I never told him anything about us." I struggle to get into the house so I can put my duffel bag down.

I cast one glance around, but I don't see Zeke. She wouldn't be yelling at me like this if he was here. I sure hope he's in the backyard so he can't hear her.

"You must have told him something!" she fires back. "He came over here to invite me to the barbecue tomorrow."

I frown at her even more deeply. "He did? In the middle of the workday?"

"Well....not *here*.....he came over to the place next door to finish the arson screen for the crime lab....."

"Oh, that." I relax considerably. I would be really worried if John came over here in the middle of his workday to invite her to the barbecue. That would be massively out of character for him.

She jabs her finger in my face. "So you knew about it! What did you tell him? Did you tell him to invite us on your behalf? Are you trying to weasel us into your community or something?"

My temper starts to flare and then my mind switches gears when I remember. She's going through something right now. She doesn't know whether she's coming or going with me.

"I didn't tell John anything everyone else in town doesn't already know, which is that you and Zeke are staying here. So he came over to do the arson screen and bumped into you. He would have invited you to the barbecue even if there was nothing going on between us....."

"THERE IS NOTHING GOING ON BETWEEN US!!" she thunders. "WHEN ARE YOU GOING TO GET THAT?!!"

I throw up both hands. "Okay. There's nothing going on between us and you and Zeke aren't going to the barbecue. You're just going to keep him all to yourself and keep him isolated from the world so he never sees other kids. You aren't going to send him to school....."

"You were the one who said keeping him out of school was a good idea!"

"I said keeping him out of school was a good idea only if you found another way for him to spend time with other kids—a safe way for him to spend time with other kids. I never said it was a good idea for you to keep him isolated because you're too insecure to face the world. And I never said it was a good idea for *you* to stay isolated because you're too insecure to face the world. That is a really terrible idea, but you already knew that. You know it in your heart, but you still won't overcome your insecurity even though you know it's best for your son—and for you."

"You have no business telling me what's best for me or my son! You and I aren't involved! You're letting me stay here because I have nowhere else to go! We aren't in a relationship! Got that?"

I throw up my hands again. "Okay. You won't get any argument from me."

Just then, Zeke comes in from the backyard. He bursts into a huge grin when he sees me. "Hey, Danny!"

"Hey, pal. Did you have a good day?"

"Yeah! Chief Brewer came over to finish the arson screen on the house next door."

"That's what your mom was just saying."

"He says you and me had epic levels of octane fumes saturated into our blood. He says Dad must have used a massive amount of gas to start the fire. He says....."

"Okay, sweetheart," Emily interrupts. "Danny doesn't want to hear all about that."

"Sure, I do." I sit down on the couch. "I want to hear all about it."

"Hey, Danny!" Zeke exclaims. "Can we keep reading *Treasure Island?*"

"You can keep reading *Treasure Island*. Go get it and you can read it to me."

He races over to the shelf to get the book. I go into the kitchen to get myself a glass of lemonade.

That's when I realize Emily is making dinner. She has three different pots simmering on the stove, something in the oven, and a cutting board laid out with a knife and a bunch of chopped vegetables.

I stand there staring at everything while I sip my lemonade. What the hell is going on here? Are we involved or not?

She keeps making such a royal case about how we aren't involved. Now she's in here cooking up a storm for me.

Is she just doing that out of gratitude for me letting them stay here....or is she trying to tell me something? Why am I reading so much into this?

I have to stick to the program. If she says we aren't involved, we aren't. Period. I won't argue with that. If she isn't ready, she isn't ready. If she says she isn't good enough for me, then she isn't.

I just have to take her at her word. If she decides she wants to be good enough for me, I'll be ready for her when she comes back to her senses.

I go back to the living room and sit down on the couch while Zeke turns to the page where he left off. He keeps reading about Jim's blood-curdling encounter with Pew and the Black Spot and the map and everything.

Zeke gets more excited the longer he reads. I find myself getting excited on his behalf. It's great to relive some of my fondest childhood memories through him.

This is why I've always liked spending time with kids. I love seeing them discover all these great memories for the first time.

He reads for a long time. I really need to go upstairs, take a shower, and change my clothes, but I can't bring myself to interrupt him.

He gets up to the part where Jim is hiding in the apple barrel listening to Long John Silver plot to mutiny against Captain Smollett. Zeke's voice shakes when he reads the part where the pirates sight land right at the most crucial part of the conversation.

Emily comes over and interrupts just then. "It's time to wash your hands for dinner, sweetie."

"No, Mom!" he counters. "This is just getting good!"

"It's gonna be good from now on, pal," I tell him. "Go wash your hands. We can read some more after dinner."

He puts the book down on the coffee table and goes to the bathroom. I go upstairs and finally change my clothes, but I don't have time to take a shower.

I get downstairs just as Emily is putting dinner on the table. She pours all three of us glasses of lemonade and then she and Zeke both bow their heads while I say grace.

I don't initiate the conversation. I don't want to step on the wrong person's toes.

"Chief Brewer invited us to the firehouse barbecue," Zeke blurts out.

I nod, but I make a strategic decision not to look at Emily. "Uh-huh. He does that."

"He does?" Zeke asks.

"Sure. He does it when someone is new to town and doesn't know anyone. I mean, he doesn't go around town inviting every new person who moves here. He usually only does it if the person has been a patient of ours and the whole fire crew knows their situation and has already been involved with the person."

I realize I probably shouldn't have used those words, but it's too late now. It isn't like Emily can get all bent out of shape about what I said. She and Zeke *are* new to town and Zeke has already been the crew's patient. They all know about her and Zeke, so technically, they are involved with the fire crew.

"Did you want to tell me the rest of what John said about the arson screen?" I prompt.

Zeke glances at his mother and decides against it. Now I really need to find out what happened between John and Emily. Whatever it was, I know for certain that it didn't have anything to do with him stepping out of line. He doesn't do that.

She must have misinterpreted what he said—kind of like she's misinterpreted everything I've said.

She was the one who came into my room last night. I definitely didn't misinterpret that. Then again, that's probably why she's acting so touchy. She's scared out of her wits.

I should just walk away and leave it alone. She is still married after all. She's right about that. I shouldn't get involved with her until she gets out of this whole Colin situation and maybe not even then.

We somehow stumble through the rest of the meal, but whatever happened between John and Emily really must have bothered both Emily and Zeke. He has trouble holding eye contact with me for the rest of the meal.

As soon as he finishes, he splits off upstairs. He doesn't stick around to read the rest of *Treasure Island*.

As soon as he leaves, Emily mumbles, "I'm sorry I accused you of talking to your brother about me. I'm sorry I jumped to the wrong conclusion."

"I meant what I said," I tell her. "If you don't want to be involved with me, it's no skin off my nose. Just don't come into my room at night anymore if that's the case. If all you need is somewhere to stay, that's fine. Just make sure it's only that and don't throw me mixed signals all the time."

I push back my chair and walk off. She can cook *and* clean tonight since I did it last night.

I go upstairs to my room to take a shower and cool down before I have to deal with anyone else. It isn't no skin off my nose if she doesn't want to get involved, but she's the one who doesn't know what she wants. She doesn't even know what's best for herself and her son.

I'm better without her until she gets clear on that.

I come out of my room planning to make myself scarce for the rest of the evening. That's when I hear Zeke in the kid's playroom down the hall.

I tiptoe over there and see him sitting on the floor. He's playing with the toys, but he doesn't look happy. He's all alone, poor kid.

I stroll in there and sit down on the bed. "Hey, pal. Do you want to read?"

He doesn't look up. "Naw. I don't feel like it."

"Is it something I said....or something John said?"

He shrugs without looking up.

"I've been meaning to ask you...." I begin. "About your dad."

"He's a monster," Zeke mumbles. "I hate his guts."

"So....you guys never had any good times together.....like we do?"

Zeke shakes his head. God, he looks devastated! Who wouldn't be with a father like that?

"Do you want to talk about it?" I ask. "Maybe you would feel better if you told someone—someone other than your mom. It doesn't have to be me. I could find you someone to talk to about it if you want to."

"I don't want to talk about it," he mumbles. "I don't want to think about it, but I have to. I always wind up thinking about it even when I don't want to."

"Well, my door is always open if you need anything. It doesn't have to be talking about it. You can just tell me if you need help with anything."

"I need other kids to play with. I've been so lonely." His voice cracks and he breaks down crying right in front of me. His shoulders rack with sobs, but he stifles the sound and holds it all inside.

My heart bleeds watching him. I can't stand seeing him in so much pain. I scoot over there to sit on the floor next to him, but as soon as I get near him, I know that isn't enough.

I put my arms around him, lift him back onto the bed, and sit him on my lap. He immediately buries his face in my neck and breaks down completely. His little body shakes with all the pain inside him trying to get out.

I can't do anything but put my arms around him and hold him. I don't have what it takes to make the pain go away. I can't do anything but be here for him. I just hope he realizes he doesn't have to go through this alone.

I'll do anything for him, but if Emily doesn't want to stay with me, she'll take him away. I don't know if I can live with that. I don't know if I can go through that again.

I don't want to hold back from him. I just want to do anything to stop her from doing that.

He cries hard for a long time. Even when he slows down and sniffs against my shoulder, I know that isn't all of it. The pain is still in there. Nothing will ever make it go away. It's too deep and he's too young to handle it all.

Without thinking, I turn and kiss the top of his head. I really do love him. I might be stupid for getting this attached so quickly, but that's just me. When I fall, I fall hard.

He doesn't take his head off my shoulder when he husks in a broken undertone, "I wish you were my dad."

"I wish that, too, buddy," I murmur and I never meant any words more. I wish he'd been with me all along and never had to go through any of this.

I can only do my best to help him, now that he has gone through it. I don't even know if I can do that, but I sure want to.

"Mom doesn't want to go to the barbecue," he croaks and starts sobbing again. "She says she won't let me go!"

"I know, buddy." I feel myself starting to get choked up from listening to him.

I hug him close while he cries. I can't do anything about Emily's decision not to go to the barbecue. Would she change her mind if she could see him right now? Does she even let herself see how much pain he's in? Maybe he hides it from her. I wouldn't be surprised.

He goes for another long time of crying. He's just starting to settle down when we hear Emily coming up the stairs.

"Zeke?" she calls. "Are you up here? It's time to get ready for bed."

He hops off my lap and bolts out of the room. "Okay, Mom!" he calls.

He dives into his room and starts scrambling to put on his pajamas. He keeps his back to the door so she won't see that he's been crying.

I slide off the bed and kneel on the floor to put the toys away. She stops in the doorway when she sees me. "He should do that."

"It's okay," I tell her. "He can do it next time."

She frowns at me, but I don't care. I keep putting the toys away and she leaves to go get Zeke ready for bed.

I finish the job and go to my room while they're both busy. I shut the door just to make it clear that I want to be alone.

I change into my pajamas and stretch out on my bed, but I have to stare at the ceiling for a long time before I straighten out my own head.

Tomorrow is Saturday. The barbecue is tomorrow. Whatever is going to happen, it better happen soon or tomorrow is not going to be a nice day for any of us.

Chapter 18: Emily

Danny comes downstairs wearing jeans, tennis shoes, and a blue windbreaker with a Fire Department logo on it. He wears a Fire Department T-shirt underneath.

"I'm going to the barbecue," he announces.

Zeke hops up from his place on the couch and hustles over to Danny. "I'm going with you."

"No, you aren't," I call from the computer desk.

I've been using Danny's desktop computer in the corner of the living room to go over both the real estate listings for rentals and the job postings around town. I haven't found anything on either account. I can't afford any of the rentals and I'm not qualified for any of the jobs.

Zeke spins around, glares at me, and snarls through gritted teeth, "Yes, I am. I'm going and you can't stop me."

I stand up to confront him. "You aren't going, Zeke. I already made my decision and that's final."

"I am so going!" He spits the words at me and turns back around to face Danny. "I'm going...so let's go."

"Zeke!" I call again in my best motherly warning tone.

He doesn't turn around. He keeps his back to me and keeps staring up at Danny. I can't read Zeke's expression—or Danny's.

Danny glances up at me and then looks down at Zeke. "I can't take you without your mom's permission. I'm sorry, but if she says no....."

"I AM SO GOING!!" Zeke screeches. "I'M GOING, DANNY!!"

"Listen, buddy....."

I can't listen to this. I walk over to them and try to take Zeke's hand.

He rips it away from me with all his strength and then actually throws a punch at me. He flies into a rage. "I'M GOING TO THE BARBECUE! I'M GOING TO THE BARBECUE!!"

I dodge the first couple of blows, and when he moves his arms out of the way, I dive in to restrain him. "Stop it, Zeke!"

Danny turns away and walks toward the door to leave. Zeke goes ballistic, throws a brutal punch that lands in my face, and charges Danny.

Zeke grabs Danny's arm and leans all the way back to stop Danny from leaving. "No, Danny! Don't leave me! You can't leave without me! I have to go! Please! You have to take me! You can't leave me here! Please don't leave me behind! I have to go!"

He screams at the top of his lungs, but his screams get all broken up with choking sobs.

Zeke holds onto Danny's hand with all his might and tries to tow Danny back into the living room. Danny doesn't move.

"Please don't leave me, Danny!" Zeke's voice cracks with agony. "Please! You know I need to go! You know I do! Please, Danny! Please!!"

Danny finally squats down in front of him. "Hey, buddy...." he begins and takes hold of Zeke's shoulders.

Before Danny can even finish what he was going to say, Zeke falls into his arms and breaks down sobbing on Danny's shoulder. "Please don't leave me!" he begs. "Please don't leave without me! I can't do this anymore!!"

Seeing him like this breaks my heart. I want to run to him. I want to be the one who holds him while he cries, but I can't even do that.

Zeke is pouring out his heart to a stranger. Zeke has barely known Danny for two weeks and Zeke is already crying out to someone else for help.

Tears spring to my eyes, mostly from the sound of Zeke's voice. I've never heard him like this. He's never cried like this in front of me. Has he been hiding this all along?

Danny holds him there, but in a second, Danny stands up still holding Zeke in his arms. Danny cradles Zeke like a baby, kisses the side of his head, and pets the hair on the back of his neck.

"Hey!" Danny murmurs. "Hey! I'm still here. I'm still here! I'm with you. I'm not going anywhere. I'm here."

I can't see them anymore through my tears. Danny isn't saying those words to me, but he would if I only let him. He would never leave as long as I wanted him to stay. He would give up everything if I needed him to.

He would do the same thing for Zeke. Danny would skip the barbecue if he thought for one instant that Zeke needed him to.

That isn't what Zeke needs and we all know it. Danny is right. I only avoided going to the barbecue because I was scared. I *am* scared. Going out among strangers in a public, social setting scares the ever-loving shit out of me.

I have to do it. I have to do it for Zeke....and for myself. That's what's best for him. I'm his mother so I have to do it no matter how much it scares me.

Danny's eyes shoot over to me and he sees tears streaming down my cheeks. He keeps murmuring under his breath to Zeke. "Hey, hey. I'm here. I'm here. I'm with you. You're with me."

Zeke is okay because he's with Danny. Zeke needs Danny. In a way, Zeke needs Danny more than Zeke needs me. I would be a really terrible mother if I took Zeke away from Danny now.

I can't look at them anymore. I turn away to the sliding glass door, and as soon as I turn my back to them, I can't hold back the tears. So much pain and fear has been building up in me all these years. I didn't let myself feel it until now.

I still hear Danny murmuring to Zeke. Zeke isn't crying as hard or as loudly, but those words keep stabbing into my brain. *I'm here. I'm here. I'm with you. I'm not going anywhere. You're with me.*

He isn't saying those words to me, but I would give anything if he was. What would it mean if he told me he wasn't going anywhere?

I don't even have to ask because he's already said them to me. He would never go anywhere if I wanted him. He would always be there the same way he'll always be there for Zeke.

Danny doesn't say those words unless he means them. I know that about him at a gut level. When he says it, he means it.

Out of nowhere, he comes up behind me and murmurs in my ear. "Come on. Let's go."

He slips his hand into mine and pulls me toward the door. I'm crying too hard even to realize what we're doing, but it sure looks like we're going.

He still carries Zeke in his other arm. Zeke lies with his head on Danny's shoulder and Zeke keeps his little arms wrapped tight around Danny's neck. Zeke clamps his eyes shut tight so he doesn't see anything.

Danny goes over to the front door and lets go of my hand for a split second while he opens the door. Then he takes my hand again, leads me out onto the porch, and lets go for another fraction of an instant to shut the door behind us.

Then he takes my hand and marches me down to the truck. He doesn't ask me for permission. We're going. It isn't a question anymore.

He parks me by the passenger door, lets go of my hand to open it, and tilts the seat forward so he can angle Zeke into the back. Danny puts Zeke in the seat and buckles Zeke's seatbelt for him.

Then Danny pushes the seat back into position, gives me one hard look, and says, "Get in."

I get in, and just like that, he bends over me and puts on my seatbelt, too. Then he shuts the door with both of us inside.

I see him doing all of this. He's taking charge of both our lives because I can't. I'm too far gone. I'm too wrecked by the past even to think straight about what's best for me.

I pull myself together while he drives through town. I don't know Howe well enough to know for certain, but it seems like he drives around for a lot longer than it should take to get across town.

I wipe the tears off my cheeks. I'm doing this. I'm going to the barbecue. I have to. Anyway, we're already on our way there.

Danny finally pulls the truck into a parking lot packed with cars. Two firetrucks are already there with their noses pointed out toward the street. Three ambulances are there, too, all lined up in a row.

Forty people crowd the beach. I spot John and Keith right away. They stand by the barbecue and try to keep their heads out of the smoke while they turn burgers and steaks on the grill.

A bunch of other people stand around in clumps while at least fifteen kids run through the waves. The kids charge up and down the beach, pause to discuss something, point to the trees in the distance, and then some of them plunge into the ocean to go swimming.

Danny parks and opens my door while I'm still sitting there staring. The whole barbecue looks so.....so inviting. Everyone out there looks relaxed like they're having the time of their lives.

Half the people here wear Fire Department or EMS uniforms, but they're all as relaxed as those in regular clothes.

Danny takes my hand and pulls me out of the truck. Then he holds the seat forward for Zeke to climb out of the back.

Zeke stands there staring at the scene, too. He doesn't move for a second.

"Well, go on," Danny finally tells him. "You wanted to come, so go have some fun."

He gives Zeke a push and Zeke bursts into a dead run heading for the other kids. He blasts past the barbecue and a few people do a double take trying to see who he is.

In an instant, he catches up with the other kids. They pause their game to surround him, but only for a second before they all race away heading for the trees.

Danny shuts the door behind me. "Just try to relax and have a good time," he tells me. "No one is here to judge or think anything about you. We're all just here to kick back and enjoy ourselves. Okay?"

He takes a cooler out of the truck bed and sets it on the pavement while he lifts out a loaded grocery bag full of chips and pretzels. He moves the bag to his left hand, picks up the cooler by its handle, and starts forward.

He says one more time, "Let's go," and we both set off walking down to the beach.

Chapter 19: Emily

D anny goes over to the picnic table, sets his cooler in the sand with seven other coolers, and puts his shopping bag on the table.

I don't know where to go, but as soon as we show up, one of the clusters of adults breaks apart and two women turn around to smile at me.

"Hey! Look who's here!" Ellen limps a few steps backward to make an opening in the circle. "How's it going? I haven't heard anything more about Zeke's head so he must be all right."

"Yeah," I mumble. "He's out there running around right now, so it looks like he's fine. Thanks for asking."

The second woman turns to me on the other side. They both maneuver themselves so I automatically get pulled into their circle.

"John says his blood screen came back positive for octane saturation." It's Leila Cunningham, the paramedic who treated Zeke the night of the fire. "That explains why he was so out of it when he didn't have a serious head injury."

"Yeah," I choke. "Thank you for everything. I really appreciate everything you did for him."

"We aren't here to talk about that," Ellen interrupts. "We're here to enjoy ourselves."

"Of course we're here to talk about that," Keith growls from the other side of the circle. "When have we ever had one of these barbecues where we talked about anything other than work? It doesn't happen."

"Ainsley says Zeke hasn't gone back to school since those assholes tried to kidnap him," another woman interjects. "You really need to talk to Jim Walker about that. The Police have procedures for at-risk kids attending school. They can put a risk management plan in place for you. I'm sure John would liaise for you if you wanted him to."

Ellen holds up her hand again. "We are definitely not talking about that! Tell us about the dog who got stuck in the trash can, Chris."

"That wasn't work-related so it isn't allowed," Keith counters.

"No, but it was funny." A third woman turns to grin at me. It's the other paramedic from the fire—the one who worked on Danny. "This dog got its head stuck in a recycling bin downtown. Once the dog got his head in there, he couldn't get out so he started clawing at it with his paws. He got both paws stuck in there, too, so his back end was sticking out while the front half of him was still buried in the recycling bin. He was a two-legged recycling bin running around the streets before Animal Control finally caught him and took the bin off "

Laughter breaks out around the circle. "I really would have liked to see that," Keith remarks.

Just then, John and Danny come over. Danny cracks the cap off a beer bottle and hands me a wine cooler. I don't even like wine coolers, but this whole experience is so.....so normal.

I didn't realize until right now just how out of the loop I've been. Danny is right. I haven't just been keeping Zeke away from real life. I've been depriving myself.

I've spent so much time isolated from the world that I don't even know how to socialize with normal people anymore. This is the destruction that Colin has wreaked on my life.

I'm only twenty-five. I should have been partying and going to college and having fun in my youth instead of being locked in a house with a child and an abusive husband.

I glance around the group. None of them acts like they know a thing about me.....and maybe they don't.

None of them acts like they know about me and Danny, either. They really do act like I'm just some new person in town who needs to meet people.

Their talk naturally turns back to work, so I can't join in the conversation. They laugh and joke about funny stuff that happened.

I can't help but admire everyone here, especially the female paramedics. They're heroes just as much as Danny is.

They're all just normal people, though. There's nothing special about them apart from their jobs. They let their hair down and fool around here, now that they aren't actually out there saving the world.

People mill around, come and go, get themselves plates of food or drinks, or go back and forth to the parking lot to get stuff from their cars. The vibe stays at this steady pulse of casual enjoyment.

The women talk about their kids and complain about household chores and errands they have to run and everyday annoyances just like all other women in the world. The men talk about their lawnmowers, their kids, their hobbies, their cars, and every other detail of their lives.

I find my gaze wandering out to the beach, but Zeke isn't there anymore. He and the other kids have disappeared somewhere, but none of the parents show any sign of being worried. None of them even looks to make sure their kids are all right.

I have to remind myself that this is a totally safe environment for Zeke. Colin won't come looking for us here. If he did, he wouldn't be able to do anything with all these tough emergency workers standing around.

I know Zeke needs to run around with other kids, but I still find it impossible to let my guard down. I want to protect him from everything even though I've never been able to protect him from anything.

The adults are still standing around shooting the bull when the kids come back. John stands next to Ellen eating a burger off a paper plate he balances in his other hand. He's stuck his beer bottle into his back pocket.

Zeke charges over to us, strips off his shoes and socks, and dumps them on the sand next to Danny. "I'm going swimming!" he announces.

Danny puts his hand into the inner pocket of his windbreaker and pulls out a pair of child-sized swimming trunks. "Put these on."

Zeke stops what he's doing to stare at the trunks. Danny dangles them in front of his eyes. They're black with a Nike logo on the leg cuff.

I stare at the trunks and then at Danny. He must have bought these trunks for Zeke even when I kept saying I wouldn't let him come to the barbecue. What else is Danny planning behind my back?

Zeke jolts out of his trance, snatches the trunks, and starts ripping at the waistband of his pants.

"Go change in the truck," Danny tells him. "And don't get sand on the carpets."

Zeke charges across the beach to the parking lot. Danny chuckles under his breath and everyone goes back to talking about something completely different.

A second later, Zeke comes barreling back down the beach wearing the trunks and nothing else. God, he looks small and frail like this! He looks so vulnerable and fragile.

He blasts races into the group of kids, and a second later, he dives up to his neck in the waves, getting tumbled around, dunked, and soaked.

Danny finishes the hot dog he's eating, and in the middle of the conversation, he goes up to the truck and comes back with a towel draped over his shoulder.

No one says a word about it. He goes and gets himself a bowl of chips and another beer. The conversation goes on as before.

I'm the only one who notices—or acts like they notice. He must have brought that towel for Zeke, too. I really need to change the way I think about.....well, everything.

Danny knows exactly what Zeke needs. Danny shows this every hour of every day. Why do I keep resisting that?

I try to distract myself by getting some food. Billy Cates is manning the barbecue. "What's your poison?" he asks me when I show up. "Your options are cholesterol, heart attack, stroke, diabetes, or kidney failure."

I have to laugh. "I'll take cholesterol and heart attack. Thanks."

He grins at me. "Good choice."

He gives me a burger and a hot dog. He's as big as Keith and just as burly, but Billy is cleaner cut—like a bigger version of John with light hair. Billy doesn't have Keith's biker vibe.

I'm in the middle of putting condiments on my food and helping myself to salad when Ellen comes over. She starts putting condiments on another burger for her daughter, Oakleigh.

"How are you doing?" she asks me again in the most casual tone possible. "Do you have a job lined up in town? The hospital has a bunch of openings. I could put in a good word for you if you need it."

"Thanks," I mutter. "I saw the listings on the Employment Office website."

She grins at me. "Is there anything more depressing than looking for a job? I went through that when I hurt my leg. You couldn't pay me to go through it again."

"Yeah, Danny told me about how you changed jobs."

I find myself studying her. She transitioned from the fire crew to the hospital. That must have been tough, but she did it. Maybe I can transition to something good, too.

She notices me watching her extra closely. "Are you okay? What do you have in mind for your next dream job?"

I turn red and look away. "I have to pass the GRE first."

"That should be easy. I'm sure you can read and write and do basic math. You should be able to pass that in your sleep."

"I hope so."

"Hey, do you want to go shopping tomorrow?" she asks me. "You could get some new clothes for yourself and Zeke. Danny has to work, but you and I could go out. You don't have to stay in the house all day every day."

She doesn't laugh when she says it. Does she even know that Colin made me stay in the house all day every day? Then I remember that she was in the hospital room when I explained that to Detective Hill.

Ellen acts like she doesn't remember me saying that. She also doesn't know that I don't have any money to buy clothes for myself and Zeke.

I just mumble, "Thanks. That would be nice."

"I was also thinking it would be good if someone—like me, for example....." She laughs at her own joke. "No, seriously. I was thinking it would be good if someone introduced you to the teachers and principal at the school. Sometimes it's hard to communicate with them if you haven't met them face to face. I know them all, so I could arrange for you to meet them and they can get to know you and find out what your and Zeke's needs are."

I only nod this time. She's being so nice, but I don't know how to deal with her. I'm a fish out of water here.

Fortunately, Zeke distracts us again by coming over to the circle. He's dripping wet and shivering with cold.

Danny grabs the towel off his shoulder, wraps it around Zeke, and rubs him to warm and dry him. Zeke tries to talk to us, but his lips are shaking too badly to form the words.

He beams with happiness, though. I've never seen him this happy and he keeps trying to break away from Danny so he can go back out there and run around some more.

Danny wraps the towel all the way around Zeke's body like a cocoon and picks him up in his arms. "Come on. You can change back into your regular clothes and then get something to eat before you go back out. You'll fall over if you don't eat something."

He carries Zeke back up to the truck. They stay there for a long time until Zeke comes racing back down the beach in his clothes. His hair is still wet, but he's much drier.

He stops at the picnic table and is grabbing handfuls of chips when Danny comes striding back from the parking lot. "Come over here to the barbecue and get some real food," he tells Zeke.

Zeke follows him. I'm starting to see Zeke as Danny's little miniature shadow. Zeke does everything Danny tells him without question.

Danny gets a burger from Billy, loads it up, and then makes Zeke sit down and eat before he goes back out to play.

I find myself fighting the urge to stop Danny from acting like Zeke's father. If everything I think about Danny, Zeke, and myself is wrong, then my instincts to protect Zeke from Danny must be wrong, too.

Zeke responds so well to Danny—almost as if Danny really is his father. Who am I to interfere with that? God knows Zeke never had much of a father in Colin.

No one in the group acts like Danny is doing anything out of the ordinary by acting like Zeke's father. No one mentions it or even seems to notice it. They act like this is all normal.....which I guess it is.

The others treat their kids the same way. The whole thing just fits together like it was meant to be. We fit together like we were meant to be—the three of us.

I really wish it could be. I really wish we could be as much a part of this family as Danny is—as they all are. I can't imagine anything better than that.

They're all so close and affectionate with each other. They share the best and worst of each other's lives. They form a little separate world all their own that no one else gets to share.

They don't act like I'm an outsider. They don't act like it would be difficult or unusual if I became part of it. They act like I'm already in it—but I would have to get together with Danny to make that happen, wouldn't I?

I'd give anything if it really could be like that, but I don't want to believe it. I don't want to get my hopes up in case something comes along and destroys it just like something always comes along and destroys every other good thing that has ever happened to me.

Chapter 20: Danny

"That was awesome!" Zeke exclaims when he climbs into the back of the truck. "Can we do it again?"

"We have these barbecues every two weeks—so not next weekend but the weekend after that. You can come then." I take a closer look at him in the cab dome light. It's getting dark outside and he's shivering again even though he's fully dressed.

I pull out of the cab, crack my emergency supply box in the truck bed, and pull out a heavy wool emergency blanket. I stick my head back inside, wrap the blanket around Zeke so his arms are all tied up inside it, and buckle his seatbelt over the top of it.

I pat him down and then, for no reason, I pat the side of his face. He beams at me. He looks so much happier now. He had a great day with the kids and I can see some of the darkness fading from his expression. That's good. He needs a whole lot more of that.

I push the passenger seat back into place and Emily gets in. "Sit tight," I tell her. "I'm gonna go down and bring up the cooler and stuff. I'll be right back."

I start the engine, turn on the heater, and shut them both in while I go down to the beach to get the rest of our stuff.

I bring up a bunch of other coolers and gear for Leila and Ellen, too. Leila kisses me on the cheek. "Have a good night, sweetheart. Drive home safely."

"You, too, darlin'." I hug and kiss Ellen. "Thanks for the great day."

"Call us if you need anything," Ellen tells me and goes over to the car where John is putting Oakleigh in the back.

I get into the cab of my truck and reverse onto the road. I have to wait for Ellis and Drew to pull the rescue truck and ambulance out first. They're on their way back to the firehouse for the end of their shift.

I switch on the headlights and drive back through town on my way home. I wind up drifting with my own thoughts and Emily doesn't say anything on the way home, either.

I don't realize until I pull into the driveway that we've driven the whole way without saying a word, but maybe that's because we're both tired.

I switch off the truck and kill the headlights. Things sound awfully quiet in the back seat, too. When I turn around, I see Zeke sound asleep in the seat. His head lolls against the seatbelt.

I chuckle under my breath. "It looks like someone really wore himself out today."

"That's good," Emily tells me. "He'll sleep like a rock tonight."

Those are the first words we've spoken to each other since I pulled into the beach parking lot. She seemed to enjoy herself today, too—as much as she can considering she didn't know anyone there.

I open her door for her and then climb into the back to unbuckle Zeke. I lift him out and he doesn't wake up when I carry him inside. He's out cold.

I put him on his bed still fully wrapped up in the blanket. He can stay like that until morning. I don't want to wake him up to make him change into his pajamas.

I linger there and let my hand run down the side of his face just because. He's such a beautiful kid. He deserves more days like today and I want to be the one to give him that. I want to make up for everything Colin did to him—and didn't do. Someone has to do it, so it might as well be me.

I go back downstairs and see the light on in Emily's room, but she keeps her door closed. That's okay. She probably wants to go to sleep.

I unload the truck and throw Zeke's towel and swimming trunks in the laundry. He really needs some new clothes and so does Emily, but I can't do anything about that tonight. I won't be able to do anything about it tomorrow, either. I have to work.

I don't want Emily wandering around town by herself—not with Colin on the loose. Maybe I'll call Jim Walker tomorrow and find out what's happening with Emily's protective order. She can't stay locked up at home all the time. She's turning out to be as much a prisoner here as she was with Colin. No wonder she's so on edge.

I put all the stuff away and start organizing my uniform and other gear for work tomorrow. I go to the kitchen, make my lunch, and leave it in the fridge so it's ready to go in the morning.

I'm getting really tired by the time I go upstairs to my room. I kick off my shoes and hang up my windbreaker when I get an email from John announcing the day and time for this month's employee meeting. Doesn't that guy ever sleep?

I sit down on the end of the bed to read the email. It's nothing I don't already know except that it includes an announcement that he'll be introducing a new hire—a new paramedic to fill the spot on the rescue truck.

That spot has been vacant since Ellen quit. This will be the twenti-
eth new hire John has brought in to try to fill the vacancy. Spectacular.
I can just imagine how well this one is going to work out.

The fire crew is starting to think that position is cursed. I guess we'll
see if the new guy can cut the mustard or not.

I throw my phone on the bed to finish getting undressed when I see
movement out in the hall. I look up.

I didn't shut my door this time. I've been living alone for so long
that I just forgot. I never shut my bedroom door because I don't need t
o.

Emily stands in the hall right outside my room. She stares at me
through the door in the same position she was in when she came into
my room last time—before I told her not to.

I freeze and stare back at her. I told her not to come into my room
if she didn't mean for us to get together. Is that why she's here? Is that
what this means?

It must mean that because she inhales a deep, shuddering breath to
bolster her resolve. Then she has to summon her courage to take one
step and enter my room. She really does know what this means.

I can't move or say anything. Is this really happening? I don't want
to trust it in case she flips out and changes her mind again.

She stands there staring down at me like it means something, but it
doesn't—not yet. She actually has to do it.

I can't take the first step—not again. I already did that and she
kicked me in the teeth.

If she wants this, she'll have to do it herself—and I mean she'll have
to do everything. She'll have to do everything to make up for the fact
that she pushed me away.

She has to brace herself before she works up the nerve to take another two steps and sit down on the bed next to me. I distract myself by picking up my belt from where I dropped it on the bed.

I wind it around my hand to coil it up. I don't know what else to do with myself until she breaks the ice.

She looks down at her hands, passes her fingers between each other, and mumbles, "Thank you for today."

"Of course," I tell her. "That's what I'm here for—to give you and Zeke whatever you need. You know that."

She doesn't look up. "I know. I'm sorry I threw that back in your face. That was wrong of me."

I put my belt aside, and since I have nothing else to do, I bend over and make a big deal about straightening my shoes and putting them one next to the other.

Now they're all ready to put away, but I don't stand up—not when she's sitting here obviously trying to tell me something important.

"I'm really grateful for what you're doing for Zeke," she murmurs. "I see what you're trying to do and I really appreciate it. He needs that from a man….I mean, from you. I wish I could be the one to give it to him, but he obviously needs it from you instead."

"He's a great kid," I tell her. "He deserves the best—a lot better than what he's gotten from Colin."

She nods down at her hands. I don't know what else to say to her. This isn't doing it—whatever it is she's trying to do by sitting here next to me. This doesn't change anything between us.

I'm just getting ready to stand up and go do my own thing when she says, "Remember when Zeke freaked out about you leaving him behind and you picked him up and you were telling him that you were here and you wouldn't go anywhere and that he was with you?"

"Yeah?" I ask. "What about it? I'll always be there for him if he needs me."

"I know." She waits way too long to say anything else. I'm just about to pull the pin on this conversation when she says, "Do you think.....do you think you could be like that for me, too?"

I look up at her and find her looking back at me with tears in her eyes. Her features tremble and her eyes swim with so much tortured emotion.

I can't believe what I'm seeing....and hearing.

"I'm sorry, Danny!" she chokes. "I don't know what I'm doing.... but I want to. I really want to, I just don't know how. You have to show me how, but I can't do this by myself anymore. I....I need you......just as much as Zeke does. I need you to tell me that you're here and that you got me and that you aren't going anywhere.....I'm such a screwup....."

I can't live with those words between us. I put my arms around her and pull her in. "You aren't a screwup, baby. It's okay. I'm here. I'm with you. I'm not going anywhere."

Her arms slip around my ribs, and just like that, she puts her head on my shoulder and starts crying in my arms. Man, she feels good! I never thought she would ever bridge that gap.

"I'm so sorry!" she howls in my ear. "I can't lose you!"

"Hey!" I murmur. "You aren't losing me. I'm right here. I'm with you. I'd do anything for you and Zeke. You know that. I can't stand the thought of you two not being here with me. That's all I want."

She breaks down sobbing for a while. I hold her until she finishes. She straightens up all businesslike and tries to pull herself together. She mumbles, "Sorry," again.

"Stop saying that," I tell her. "It's gonna take some time for you to get over this whole Colin disaster."

"I'm still married to him. You know that, right?"

"Yeah, I know."

She looks up at me and those eyes burn with so much pain. She's in as much pain as Zeke, which means I need to take care of her just as much as I need to take care of him.

That was my mistake—thinking she didn't need me. I never should have pulled away from her. I shouldn't have hardened myself against her.

This was just her way of dealing with the pain. I should have realized that she's hurting just as much as he is. She needs just as much attention and care. That's my job now.

"Do you want to....." she rasps. "Do you want to wait.....until I'm not married to him anymore?"

"No, baby," I tell her. "I don't want to wait for anything."

She nods down at her hands. She doesn't know how to bridge the gap. That's what this is. It isn't because she doesn't want to be with me. She just doesn't know how.

I have to remind myself how young she is. She's been frozen in time since she was seventeen. Colin hardly even let her talk to anyone in the last seven years. She doesn't know how to do anything.

Chapter 21:
Danny

I cup Emily's chin and kiss her. Her lips taste like salt and they don't respond the way they did before.

I need to do something to cross the divide between us. We can't just keep sitting here.

I stand up and shut the bedroom door. She stays perched on the edge of the bed and fidgets, now that she knows what this means. She's in my bedroom and she'll stay here from now on.

I want to change into my pajamas, but that seems like a step too far considering how bad things have gotten these last few days. I put my shoes away and then stretch out on the bed fully clothed. She's still fully clothed, too.

"Come here, baby," I tell her. "Lie down."

She lies down and curls up next to me. I wrap my arm around her shoulders and she rests her head on my chest.

"What are we going to do?" she half-whispers.

"I'm gonna get up and go to work tomorrow. I'm going to call Jim Walker about your protective order and find out how the arson investigation is coming along and how soon we can expect the Police Department to take Colin into custody. Once we know that, we can work on filing your divorce paperwork and maybe put a risk management plan in place so Zeke can start going to school again."

She heaves a trembling sigh and nods against my chest. "Okay."

I kiss the top of her head and go back to lying quietly with her. I don't need it to be any different.

She finally breaks the silence by murmuring, "I wish it could have been like this from the beginning."

"I wish that, too, baby, but we needed this to happen so we could find each other. You wouldn't have moved to Howe if not for this. It's a good thing and now we can make up for all that lost time."

"Yeah," she breathes. "You're right."

"I want you to take Zeke downtown and get yourself and him a new set of clothes and maybe shoes—whatever else you need—but I don't want you to go alone. Maybe I'll ask Leila to take you on her next day off."

Her head shoots up and she stares at me. "Did you tell her that?"

"Who—Leila?"

"Did you tell her you wanted her to take me shopping?"

"No. I just thought of it right now."

She puts her head back down on my chest and sighs.

"Why do you ask? Did something happen at the barbecue? I thought you had a good time today."

"Ellen," she mutters. "Ellen offered to take me shopping. Tomor row....while you're at work."

"Oh." I frown to myself. "Well, I didn't have anything to do with that, but if she's taking you, I'll give you some money to buy what you need."

She doesn't answer. I don't know what else to say to her, but this is good. She's talking now.

I can keep doing this forever if I have to. This is what I wanted—she and I arranging our future together with Zeke. This is my dream coming true right here.

I'm tired from today, though, so I stretch out my arm and switch off the bedside lamp. Darkness falls over the room and here we are, lying together in our bedroom—the bedroom she and I will share from now on.

I start to drift off when she moves her head onto my shoulder. She doesn't move anything else.....and then her arm slides forward. Her hand glides onto my stomach....and her fingers flex into my midsection-
.

It happens in a split second—just long enough to give me a charge of heat rushing to my crotch. She means *that.* She wants *that.* She wants us to be like that—not just together in this room to sleep together and arrange our future together. She wants all of it.

My eyes snap open, but before I can do anything, she rolls on top of me, straddles me, presses her breasts into my chest, and starts kissing me.

She doesn't attack me in a ravenous frenzy the way we did last time. It's always been like that between us, but not now.

Just as much burning passion and desire smolders on her lips. Her tongue sizzles with just as much electricity, but this time, I feel a depth of emotion in that kiss that wasn't there before.

She runs her fingers through my hair, strokes my cheeks, and massages the back of my neck while she buries her tongue in my mouth. Her body surges on top of me and she rotates her hips in madding circles on my crotch.

She doesn't tear me apart and throw herself at me, though. She does just enough to show me how much she wants me. She doesn't push me to do anything I don't want to do. This is just us together.

My hands stroke up her sides to her breasts and down to her beautiful round hips. I follow her rhythm and pull her down harder on my spike, but this feels so warm and delicious and....close. We're together. We don't have to hurry up and do it before someone finds out.

We don't have to hurry up and do anything because we're going to be doing this for a long, long time. We don't have to stay up all night grappling every breath and smell from each other. Those things are already ours.

Her body trembles faster and deeper with every passing second, but she still doesn't escalate. She just stays there to make sure I know what she's doing. She doesn't plan to do anything other than kiss me with our bodies connected like this. If we do anything else, it's up to me.

I crush her breasts through her shirt and feel the same rush of hot breath coming from her nostrils. Her body quivers with tension and desire. I love the way she shows me how much she wants it.

I thread my fingers into her hair and use it to steer her mouth into mine. Her head turns from side to side consuming me in so much wet softness. Her mouth tastes amazing.

I'm too hard to stop now. I want so much of her, but I don't want to break the spell.

I push her off me and make her sit up. She stays straddling me and runs her hands up and down my chest. Her eyes smoke with passion and sadness and fear and longing all mixed up at the same time.

She doesn't break eye contact when I start unbuttoning her shirt. She holds me there and lets me see just how scared she is. Her face wrenches with buried agony. She knows what she's doing and it terrifies her, but she does it anyway. She does it for me.

I unbutton her shirt and she shrugs out of it when I slide it off her shoulders. She looks absolutely magnificent riding me like this in nothing but her bra.

Faint light from the streetlight outside shines on her shoulders, cleavage, her narrow waist, and her hair. Her eyes sparkle with all the desire seething in their depths.

I stroke her chest and shoulders. I trace the lace edging in her bra straps plunging to her cleavage. I run my fingertips over the outside of the cups to tease her. I get another surge of adrenaline when her nostrils flare and her eyes float half-shut.

Those eyes drift open to seize me again and she rakes her fingertips down my chest and stomach to my waistband. She pulls up my shirt and then her hot, delicate hands come to rest on me.

She touches my chest and tugs my shirt farther up until I sit up to take it off. She helps me and then throws the shirt aside.

I lie back to gaze up at her and now her hands match mine in exploring my chest, stomach, and shoulders. She keeps touching my face, running her fingers down my neck, and her eyes gleam with all the desire in her heart. I see it shining out at me.

I hold out my hand to touch her face and she falls into me kissing me for the ages. Her hair spills over my face and into my hands. Her warm breath fills me with so much happiness. I never want to stop kissing her.

She rides me harder and faster. Her deep panting breaths turn to little excruciating moans every time she pumps her hips against me. She needs it and so do I. We both need this to seal what's happening between us.

I get busy on her jeans, but I only get as far as unzipping her zipper. I want all of her right now even though I know I can get her anytime I want.

I shove my hand down inside her soaking wet panties. She adjusts her position and slams herself down on my fingers.

She screams and her body explodes, but our kisses muffle the noise. I pull her into my mouth to silence her while her slippery ooze gushes onto my hand.

She rides my hand hard screaming again and again in my mouth. Her body convulses and her inner muscles tremble with the intensity of that climax.

She collapses on top of me, but she doesn't stop pumping into my fingers. The tension in her doesn't slacken in the slightest. She can just keep going forever.

I want so much more of her than this, so I pull my hand out and push her jeans down. She kicks them away and then sits up on her knees to take her bra off.

I take that opportunity to swivel my feet onto the floor and take my own pants off. Once I get into that position, I don't want to lie down again.

I pull her onto my lap to straddle me again and she wraps her thighs around me with her knees bent up.

She stares into my eyes at close range while we kiss endlessly. I can't stop staring into those eyes. I see my whole future in them. This is my woman. That boy down the hall is my boy. No one will ever take them away from me. No way in hell. I'll kill anyone who comes between us.

She doesn't look away. She stares all the way back into me and those eyes claim me as hers. I'm her man. I'm the man who will give her and Zeke a life. I'm the man who will keep this family going and make sure nothing interferes with what we have.

Those eyes tell me she knows it as well as I do. The rest is just details. We can handle the details. I can face anything that comes. I want to. I've never wanted anything more than this.

I slide my hand up to the back of her neck. She gasps and her eyes lose focus for a second when I grab her hair.

Then she drags her eyes open again to lock on me with insatiable passion. She loves that. She loves me commanding her and steering her where I want her to go. She loves me taking control and conquering her. She gives herself to me as never before.

Her mouth sags open and she widens her thighs to take me inside. She rides down on me and now neither of our bodies will be denied. She devours my mouth and pants in craven lust when I pull her away by the hair.

I hold her at a distance and watch her burning up with aching desire. She keeps glancing down at my mouth and trying to get to me. I play with her by holding her off, but no force on Earth can stop her hips from driving down on me again and again.

She wavers there in my hands. Her desire beats through her to make our bodies join. Every thrust squishes another burst of hot, sizzling honey all over me. Mmm. Yes. That's so good. I need this so bad.

I want to move back over to the bed. I want to do so many things with her. I don't know what to do first.

I stand up to swivel her onto her back, but once I get to my feet, I stop there. I hold her up with both arms under her ass while she rides me. She straps her arms and legs around me and kisses me while I hold her.

Holding her like this gives me an unstoppable feeling of ultimate power. I can do anything. I can do no wrong. The whole world exists just for me and her and Zeke.

She keeps pumping down on me without a break. She'll keep going like this until I tell her to stop.

I turn to the bed, and just because, I throw her down on the mattress. She bounces with a shriek, and before she can sit back up or even stop bouncing, I grab her and flip her onto her hands and knees.

She shoots me a look of volcanic, animal desire over her shoulder and moans when I pull her hips back toward me. She arches her back and spirals her hips in front of me to lure me in.

I ease her back into me, but I don't want to stay like this. She's too far away.

Every position is outstanding and so full of hungry yearning bliss. I can take any of them. Each one expresses a shade of our desire for each other. Each one is true and good in its own way.

She throws back her head and her hair spills across her back and shoulder. She looks mouth-watering like this. Does she want me to pull her hair again? Does she want me to hold onto the back of her neck and slam her into next week?

I grab her hair, but in the end, I wind up using it to pull her upright onto her knees. I wrap my arms around her from behind, slide my hand up her neck to hold onto her jaw, and control the movement of her body beating down on me.

I press my mouth against her ear so she can hear me growling all my need and hunger into her brain. I want her to hear me rutting for her. I want her to hear me growling over her as her alpha.

She gasps and whines. She cocks her hips back to position herself perfectly to take my thrusts. She yelps with every stroke and her sodden wetness clamps me in a death grip.

I slide my other hand between her legs and the feeling of her dissolving in another torrential climax blasts me into outer space. I explode into her, but the tension doesn't ease. If anything, it just keeps building.

It will just keep building forever. That energy will carry us through every obstacle that lies in front of us. Nothing will be able to stop us as long as we have each other.

Chapter 22: Emily

I drift out of a sound sleep when I feel Danny stir in the bed next to me. It's still dark outside.

I'm about to go back to sleep when he grabs my leg, pulls me onto my back, and before I even fully wake up, he crawls between my legs and buries his face in me.

I whimper as the tension brings me fully awake and then a rush of pleasure lulls me back into a drunken sea of bliss. He adjusts his position under the covers and wraps his arms around my thighs to pull me into his mouth.

I moan and writhe on the bed, but he doesn't let me go. I'm still sensitive and trembling from last night. That sensitivity makes me escalate much faster now.

His fingers glide inside me and the pleasure spirals to the breaking point. I convulse as the tension spikes out of control and then I erupt all over his face. I grab his hair and ride his mouth until the last epic ripples fade out of me.

He leaves me intoxicated with so much pleasure that I can't think straight. I start to fade back into sleep when he crawls out from under the covers, lies down next to me, and turns me to face him.

I don't know if I'm dreaming or awake when he starts kissing me. I wind my arms around his neck and run my fingers through his hair, but that rock-hard spike throbbing between my legs tells me he isn't interested in sleep.

How does he stay so hard when we've already done it so many times? He picks up my leg, hooks my knee over his elbow, and drives in at an angle.

I collapse back, but he holds me in position while he drills in to the hilt. "Danny!" I moan.

"That's right, baby," he growls. "You know who this is taking you right now."

My eyes swim back into focus and I look into those eyes glaring back at me. "Danny....please....."

"Beg me for it, baby," he snarls. "Beg me to own you this way."

I would beg him for it, but I'm too out of my mind with all the pleasure he's giving me. I moan again.

He clamps his hand in my hair and pulls my head up. "Look at me, baby. Look at me and let me see how much you want this."

My body obeys his commands without me even trying. My eyes float open and I can't look away. I have trouble focusing on him. I have to concentrate to hold his gaze. I need him to see me like this. I need him to see me spasming for him and falling apart in his hands.

He snatches a kiss from my lips and his thrusts pick up speed as he drives in harder.

His chest and stomach tighten with the effort. He clamps his hand harder on my head and he winds up pulling me down on his chest. I buckle there and screams take me as we both explode into each other.

I shut my eyes and howl into that hollow place in his chest. His heart is in there. His heart understands that I'm broken in my need for him.

He kisses the side of my head and his fingers ease in my hair. He nudges me up to kiss me and then pulls me against him so I can huddle in his arms.

I must have passed out from exhaustion because I wake up in full daylight when he sits down on the edge of the mattress. He pushes the hair out of my eyes and kisses me lightly on the lips.

He's already wearing his uniform and his hair is wet from taking a shower. "Come downstairs and eat some breakfast," he tells me. "I need to go to work pretty soon, so you'll need to get out of bed and function today."

"Do I have to?" I grumble.

He laughs. He looks so happy that I open my eyes the rest of the way so I can see him.

He beams down at me with a huge, glowing smile. "Yes, you have to. You're a mother, remember?"

"How could I forget?" I mutter.

He laughs again and leans all the way over me so his face comes right up close to mine. "I love you," he murmurs. "I love you and Zeke like my own. I'm gonna give you everything."

I wrap my arms around him and pull him down to kiss him. "I love you," I whisper into his ear. "I don't want anything but for us to be together like this."

He falls into kissing me, but he tears away all too soon. He stands up and leaves me lying in bed.

He goes over to the closet. "You can wear my bathrobe. You've been wearing the same clothes since the fire, so at least put them through the laundry before you do anything else. Once I get to the firehouse, I'll text Ellen about taking you and Zeke downtown today."

He lays a fluffy white bathrobe across the foot of the bed and leaves. I take a shower, wind my wet hair into a bun, and put the robe on. I put my clothes in the washing machine before I go into the living room.

Zeke is already sitting at the table eating breakfast while Danny serves him. Zeke is fully dressed—unlike me.

Zeke doesn't act like me showing up to the breakfast table like this is in any way out of the ordinary. If he heard me and Danny last night, Zeke doesn't show it.

Danny puts a plate of scrambled eggs, bacon, and toast in front of me. Then he pours me a cup of coffee. He's just moving the milk and sugar closer to my plate when his phone rings.

He takes the call in the kitchen and talks to someone in one-word sentences before he hangs up.

He comes back to the dining room. "That was Jim Walker. The warrant just went out for Colin Montgomery's arrest. They'll be taking him into custody as soon as they find him."

He goes over to Zeke and kisses him on the top of the head. Then he comes around to my side and kisses me on the top of the head right in front of Zeke.

"I gotta go," Danny tells us. "You two stay out of trouble today. I'll see you later."

He leaves me sitting there staring at Zeke. Zeke looks back at me, but I can't read in his expression if he thinks that kiss meant anything. Danny kissed me exactly the same way he kissed Zeke. Does Zeke have a clue what that means?

Zeke breaks eye contact first and goes back to eating his breakfast. I look down at my plate.

That's the moment when I realize just how little I've been eating in....well, years. I've hardly eaten at all the whole time I've been with Colin.

I do eat, but not enough. I'm usually too nervous to eat.

I can't let this food go to waste. Danny made this breakfast for me and Zeke. I couldn't disrespect Danny by not eating it.

I eat it and drink my coffee. Zeke excuses himself and goes outside to play while I put my clothes in the dryer.

I clean the kitchen while I wait for them to dry. I don't want Ellen to show up and see me wearing dirty clothes. It's bad enough I've been wearing the same jeans and shirt for more than a week.

I change my clothes, and when I come downstairs, I spot Zeke sitting on the couch reading *Treasure Island*. I smile at him. He isn't waiting for Danny to come home. Zeke is reading ahead to find out what happens.

I turn away to the desktop computer to go over the job listings from the Employment Office.

I check my email and find a bunch of notifications from the real estate listings. I smile at them, too. I can delete them all. I don't need another place to live. I already have one.

I sit down at the desk, but instead of searching for a job, I wind up looking out the window at the backyard. I live here with Danny now.

I should tell Zeke. I should explain to him that Danny and I are becoming a couple and that Zeke and I won't be leaving this house.

He'll be thrilled. He'll be over the moon when he finds out that Danny and I are getting together. Zeke loves Danny as much as I do—maybe even more.

Thinking about them makes my stomach flip. Danny is everything Zeke needs in a father figure. I wish Danny was Zeke's real father. I wish I hadn't wasted the last seven years with Colin, but like Danny says, we wouldn't be together now if not for this.

I might have other kids with Danny by now, but I wouldn't have Zeke. I'm glad I have him. I wouldn't want another kid.

My head swivels around and I watch him across the room. He's always wanted siblings. Danny and I can have more children of our own. Zeke would love that.

I find myself smiling at him while I daydream about our future together. He doesn't know. He doesn't know how wonderful our life is going to be now that we found Danny.

I sigh with pleasure when I think about it, but before I can turn back to the computer, the front door explodes off its hinges.

I stare in stark horror as my husband Colin storms into the house. He hasn't cut his brown hair. It hangs much longer over his eyes a thick mat of stubble covers the bottom part of his face.

He wears a knee-length blue trench coat over a suit with no blazer. He's even wearing a tie and polished leather shoes. He never dressed like this before. His clothes don't look right compared to his disheveled appearance and the crazed look in his wild blue eyes.

His gaze darts around the living room and he levels a gun at me across the house. He takes two steps into the living room, spots Zeke, and swivels the gun in that direction.

Zeke screams and dives behind the couch to hide. Colin instantly corrects and turns the gun toward me.

I shoot off my chair, but he invades the house so fast that he gets to me before I can fully stand up.

He fires the gun at me once and deliberately misses. The bullet crashes through the glass sliding door behind me, and before I can get away, he grabs me.

He shoves me by the shoulder hard enough to slam my chair down on the floor with me still on it. In a heartbeat, he bends over me with the gun pointed straight in my face.

"Did you think you could get away from me?!!" he thunders. "Did you think you could take my son away from me?!"

I open my mouth to answer, but he punches me hard enough to stun me. I don't have time to recover before he grabs me by the hair and drags me to my feet.

"You thought you could get away from me!!" he roars. "You thought you could just leave me because you wanted to!" He slams me down on the table, yanks me onto my back, and aims the gun in my face again. "No one takes what's mine! Understand?! NO ONE TAKES WHAT'S MINE!!"

"I'm not yours and neither is Zeke!!" I shriek. "You don't own us!! We aren't your prisoners anymore!!"

He grabs me by the shirt collar, hauls me off the table, and slams me down hard before he jams the gun barrel right into the bridge of my nose. "You die!" he snarls in my face. "You don't want to be mine anymore? You leave me when you die—both of you!"

"I hate you, Colin!" I bellow. "You can kill me, but you'll never make me love you—and you'll never make Zeke love you! You're a monster!"

"YOU BITCH!!" he roars. "I'll kill you for that!"

He straightens up with his left hand still clamped on my shirt. He uses his fist to pin me down on the table, locks his right elbow to hold the gun at arm's length, and his knuckles whiten on the trigger as he tightens his grip to shoot me in the head.

I don't care anymore. I love Danny. I'll die loving him. I gave him my all. No one can ask anything else of me. At least I'll die knowing I did everything so we could be together.

Colin's eyes go hard and cold. He clamps his lips together in a furious scowl of determination. He really is going to kill me.

At that moment, someone steps behind him out of nowhere. I have half a second to see Danny materialize behind Colin.

Danny grabs Colin by the back of his trench coat, rips Colin away, and sends him staggering across the living room. Colin slams into the fireplace and knocks all of Danny's decorations to the floor, but Colin doesn't notice.

He lunges to his feet, aims his gun, and fires at me. Danny steps in front of me at the last second and jerks to one side when the bullet strikes him. "DANNY!!" I scream.

Zeke screams out at the same time, but Danny doesn't fall. He stays where he is even when Colin charges him.

Colin tries to dodge around Danny to get to me, but Danny moves just as fast and the two men collide in a ground-shaking thump.

Colin's weight topples Danny into the armchair and they both hit the floor. "DANNY!!" I scream and so does Zeke.

Zeke huddles behind the couch—right where he can see Colin and Danny wrestling all over the floor.

I rush over there to help Danny, but he yells, "Stay back!" over his shoulder.

I stop dead in my tracks and see him and Colin fighting over the gun. Both men lock their hands around the weapon and jerk each other back and forth trying to get it away from each other.

Neither of them can yank it out of the other's grip. They toss and throw each other over and under each other more than once. They crash into the coffee table and bump into the couch.

Zeke screams again. "GET OUT OF HERE, ZEKE!!" Danny roars.

Zeke screeches, scuttles backward, and scoots around the other side of the couch, but when he gets there, Danny and Colin wind up rolling to that end of the living room, too.

Colin gives one more hellacious yank and slams Danny down on his back. "DANNY!!" Zeke shrieks.

I can't move, not even to tear my eyes away from Colin moving the gun just a little closer to Danny's head. The two men pin the gun between both their chests. Danny's muscles strain under his T-shirt trying to force the gun away from his own chin.

Colin rears up on his arms and his mouth splits in a lunatic grin of murderous triumph as he shoves the gun barrel under Danny's jaw. If the gun goes off right now, it will blow Danny's head off.

Colin gives a sick laugh and then grits his teeth. His wrists strain as he puts just a little more pressure on the trigger.

Zeke screams out one last time, "DANNY!" Sobs choke that scream. We can both see it's hopeless.

At the last second before the gun goes off, Danny gives Colin's arm an almighty wrench. The gun flips up and fires into the crease between Colin's neck and the underside of his jaw.

His head evaporates in a cloud of blood and he topples right on top of Danny. Danny barely has the strength to push Colin's body off.

Chapter 23: Emily

Colin's body topples off Danny and rolls onto the floor, but Danny just lies there gasping and groaning. Wet, dark blood saturates the side of his shirt.

I charge over to him just as Zeke comes around the couch and falls on his knees by Danny. "Danny!!" we both scream. "Danny!!"

He coughs once. "Baby......call.....911....."

Zeke rounds on me and screams in my ear. "Call 911, Mom!! Call 911!"

I charge back to the table and grab the extra phone Danny has left for me to call him if I need him.

I nearly drop the phone in my frenzy to dial the numbers. Zeke bends over Danny practically screaming in Danny's face. "You're gonna be okay, Danny! You have to be! We'll call the paramedics! They'll take you to the hospital! Mom is calling 911! You're going to be okay! I promise!"

"Buddy....." Danny chokes. "Are you.....okay.....? Did he....hurt you......?"

Zeke doesn't hear him. "You're gonna be okay, Danny! You're gonna be okay!! You have to be!!"

Just then, the phone answers on the other end and a man's voice startles me out of my wits. "911 emergency dispatch. Please state the nature of the emergency."

"We need an ambulance—right away!" I hear myself bellowing into the phone, but I can't stop myself. "Someone......someone's been shot......Two people......and we need the Police......and an ambulance....."

"I'm dispatching Police and ambulance crews now, Ma'am," the dispatcher replies. "I just need you to confirm your address......"

I blunder through the rest of the conversation, but I only get halfway through it when Police Chief Jim Walker comes racing up to the front door. It's been standing open all this time and he walks right in.

He wears a suit and he must have been coming over to talk to me about Colin's arrest warrant. He takes one look at the mess on the living room floor. "Holy shit!" he exclaims and yanks out his phone, but right then, I hear sirens in the distance.

In minutes, the whole fire crew invades the house and surrounds Danny. Leila tries to pull Zeke away, but he rushes Danny and attacks him again. "You're gonna be okay, Danny! The ambulance is here! You're gonna be okay!"

Danny smiles at Zeke, but Danny has to fight to keep his eyes open. He raises his other hand and squeezes the side of Zeke's head once. "I'm okay, buddy. I'm okay. Go with your mom. I'll be okay."

Leila succeeds in pulling Zeke away and then she and the other paramedics block my view of Danny. Zeke backs off and I wrap my arms around him from behind to pull him against me.

We both watch the paramedics work on Danny. Leila starts an IV and Chris Daniels shines a light in his eyes while she fires a million questions at him.

The paramedics give orders to the firefighters to load Danny onto a backboard and gurney. The two women call information back and forth to each other about everything they're doing.

Keith and Billy lift the gurney onto its wheels and steer Danny out of the house. Zeke and I go out onto the porch to watch them load Danny into the ambulance, but before we get there, Detective Hill and Chief Walker come over to us.

"We need you to step out of the house, Ma'am," Chief Walker tells me. "The forensics team needs to come in and gather evidence and the Medical Examiner needs to remove the body. Detective Hill and I need to take both your statements, so if you don't mind stepping outside...."

He gestures toward the front door. No one has shut it.

Part of the door jamb hangs loose where Colin forced his way into the house. The whole living room lies in ruins. I want to clean it up and make it the way it was before, but I can't do that.

Crime lab technicians in white lab coats pour into the house. They cover the whole living room and start spraypainting a line around Colin's body on the carpet.

I can't watch this. I take Zeke's hand and we walk outside. The ambulance is already disappearing around a corner down the block. Danny is gone.

Chief Walker and Detective Hill lead me and Zeke off by ourselves and take our statements about everything that happened. The Fire Department leaves, so it's just the forensics team and the Police swarming all over and inside Danny's house.

The place looks like a war zone with my burned-out property right next door. Did I do this? I leave a path of destruction everywhere I go and now Danny has gotten hurt again because of me.

"Will we be able to keep living here?" I ask Chief Walker when he finishes taking my statement.

"Oh, sure," he tells me. "You and your son can go back inside as soon as the forensic team finishes."

"Don't you have to tape off the house?" I ask. "Isn't the whole house a crime scene?"

He makes a face. "I don't think there's any question about this being self-defense, Ma'am. We had a warrant for the deceased's arrest on two counts of attempted murder against you and your son. Danny has a gunshot wound to the chest and the dead man still had his own finger on the trigger when he got shot. I think this case is pretty cut and dried. If something in the forensics report comes back wonky, you'll be the first to hear about it. In the meantime, you can go back inside once they finish."

He and Detective Hill leave to coordinate the Police presence around the neighborhood. I stand there resting my hands on Zeke's shoulders and we both stare at Danny's house.

That house gave us our one hope for a better life. Now it's a crime scene just like the rest of my disastrous life.

Zeke and I can't even go back inside because there are too many Police personnel in there. How long will this take? We might have to stand out here all day.

Just then, a passenger car pulls up at the corner down the block. All the kids on the school playground gather at the school's outermost perimeter to watch what's going on.

The car door opens and Ellen gets out. She has to lock her leg brace before she limps down the sidewalk coming closer.

She exchanges a few words with the officers standing guard around the scene. Then she hobbles over to me and Zeke.

"Come on over to my car and I'll drive you to the hospital," she tells me. "This could take all night and you'll want to be there for Danny. Come on."

She leads me and Zeke to her car. "Thank you for this," I tell her.

"Cut it out," she counters. "We're family. Get in."

She pulls the seat forward so Zeke can climb in the back. Then I get into the passenger seat and she takes the wheel.

"Is Danny okay?" Zeke asks from the back.

"I don't know. I didn't hear," Ellen calls over her shoulder. "I just got the call from John. He told me you two probably needed a ride to the hospital. The rest of the crew is already there."

"You mean….everybody?" I stammer.

She shoots me a look before she goes back to driving. "We're family, darlin'. That means all of us. Whoever is on duty will stay at the hospital as long as they can until they either get another callout or John tells them to go back to the firehouse. No one wants to leave when one of our own is in danger."

"He better be okay," Zeke croaks from the back seat. His voice shakes.

"Danny's tough," Ellen tells him. "He's gotten hurt way worse than this and come through just fine. Just remember the fire. He did all that and still bounced back. You can't keep that guy down. You can't keep any of the Brewers down. They were all born tough. Here we are."

She pulls into the hospital parking lot and we all get out. We have to walk slowly to keep up with Ellen, but it pays off in the end.

She knows everyone in the hospital and finds out right away where Danny is. We ride the elevator and walk into a waiting room packed with everyone from the firehouse.

"He's in surgery," John tells us. "He isn't in any danger, though. They just had to sew up the damage to his shoulder."

"You promise he's gonna be okay?" Zeke demands. "You're sure?"

"I'm sure," John replies. "I would never lie to you about something like that."

I pull Zeke away. "Come on, sweetie. Let's sit down. We could be here for a while."

We sit down in the chairs, but we're the only ones who do. Everyone else stands around for hours while they wait for news about Danny.

I find myself watching them. Keith paces on one side of the room. Leila stands near him, but she doesn't stop him from pacing.

The other firefighters shuffle their feet and keep checking their watches. Chris and two other female paramedics stand in a corner talking about Danny's injuries. John works on his phone the whole time.

Ellen stays standing for an hour. Then she sits down next to us and unlocks the knee joint on her leg brace so she can bend her leg.

She waits another two hours before she stands up, murmurs something to John, and leaves. He only nods and doesn't look up from his phone.

After five hours of waiting, a doctor in green scrubs comes out and gives us the word. "He's sleeping in recovery. He's out of danger and he's going to make a full recovery. You don't need to wait anymore. No one will be going in to see him until morning anyway. You might as well all go home and get some sleep."

John shoves his phone in his pocket, approaches the doctor, and shakes his hand. "Thank you."

"Forget it," the doctor replies. "It wouldn't be a day at the office without Danny Brewer on the table."

No one laughs. Keith shakes the doctor's hand next and thanks him.

Before I can stop him, Zeke goes over there, shakes the doctor's hand, and thanks him, too.

"You're welcome," the doctor replies. "Danny is going to be fine. I've seen him much worse than this. Now go home."

He leaves and John turns to the rest of the crew. "You heard the man. Second crew, head back to the firehouse. The rest of you—get out of here. We'll meet back here in the morning and then Danny can bore us all with his jokes the way he always does."

The others mutter to themselves. John turns to me. "You two come with me and I'll give you a ride home. Jim Walker says the Police are done with the house."

He leads us outside and goes through exactly the same routine that Danny does when we get in his truck. John pulls the passenger seat forward so Zeke can climb into the back. Then John holds the door until I get into the passenger seat before he closes it for me.

He starts the engine and drives us back to Danny's house. "You call me if you need anything," he tells me when he lets us out in the driveway. "If either of you feels uncomfortable staying here, you call me and you can stay at my place until we work out another solution for you. I mean it."

"Thank you," I tell him. "I can't tell you how grateful I am for all your help."

"The nightmare is over. You can sleep tonight."

He drives off. Zeke and I stand in the driveway watching him out of sight. Then Zeke turns up his eyes to look at me. "Mom?"

"Yeah, sweetheart?"

"Is it true? Is Dad really gone?"

"You saw him, sweetheart. He tried to kill me again and Danny shot him."

"I know, but......" He stares out at the neighborhood. He can see the deserted school from here. "I don't know if I can ever believe he's really gone."

"Let's go inside. We can't spend the night out here."

We walk up to the front door, but we both have to stop there and stare inside at the wreckage of the living room.

The spraypainted outline of Colin's body stands out against the carpet. The massive bloody stain near the outline's head would have given it away more than anything that someone got shot and killed here. The outline doesn't mean nearly as much as that stain.

Zeke crosses the threshold first, walks around the outline to the fireplace, and picks up Danny's frame full of decorations.

The glass has smashed out of the frame, but the decorations are still pinned to the black velvet backing.

Zeke uses his hand to brush the broken glass off the mantel and sets the frame back in its place. Then he picks up the picture of John and the mayor presenting Danny with the Medal of Valor.

Zeke sets the picture up on the mantel even though it doesn't have a frame anymore. Zeke lays the decorated cross flat on the mantel in front of the picture. "He's a hero. He saved both our lives again."

"Yes, he is. Now we can do something for him by making the house as nice as we can before he comes home. Come and help me clean this place up. Chief Walker said the forensics people don't need anything else from this place. Come to the dining room. I'll make you some dinner and then we'll work to get this place ready for Danny to come h ome."

Zeke follows me without a word of complaint. I warm up some leftover cannelloni for both of us. We eat quickly and then get to work.

I vacuum the carpet and Zeke straightens the coffee table. He wipes up splattered blood and we use stain remover on the couch cushions.

Then he stands back and stares down at the outline of Colin's body. "What are we going to do about that?"

"There's nothing we can do about it. That stain and the spray paint are going to be there forever. I can't afford to replace the carpet. We would need another piece of carpet to cover this and we don't have that. We'll just have to leave it there until we come up with some other way to cover it up."

Zeke jumps, gasps, and spins around. "Mom!"

"What, sweetie?"

"I know where we can find some carpet!"

I frown at him. "You do?"

"Yeah! No one is using it. Come on!"

He drags me out to Danny's garage. Sure enough, Zeke shows me a big roll of grey carpet stashed in a corner of the garage.

"It's the same carpet that's on the stairs," Zeke tells me. "Maybe Danny had extra and decided to keep it."

"This is perfect, sweetheart. Help me take it into the living room."

We spend the next few hours lugging the carpet into the living room. Both Zeke and I nearly break ourselves in half doing that job. He's too small to help me very much. We finally collapse when we lay it along one edge of the living room.

"Now we have to move the couches, coffee table, and chairs," Zeke tells me.

I want to tell him to leave the job until morning. It's already seven o'clock at night.

He gets up right away and starts throwing his weight against the couch to move it out of the way. He doesn't quit until I get up and help him.

We puff and sweat for another hour to move the furniture, roll out the extra carpet, yank it into position, and then heave all the furniture back into place.

We both collapse on the couch when we finish. "We'll leave the rest for tomorrow," I pant.

Zeke casts a critical gaze around the living room. "This looks nice. This looks nice enough for Danny to come home."

I find myself beaming at him. "Sweetie....I have to tell you something."

He looks up. "What is it? Is it something bad?"

"No, darlin'. It's something good. Danny and I.....are going to be together. You and I are going to live here....with Danny. We aren't going to find another place to live. We're going to stay here and be a family with him."

Zeke's jaw drops. I expect gasps and exclamations about how cool that is.

Instead, he bursts into tears and throws his arms around me. He sobs for a long time. "Thank you, Mom!" he wails. "Thank you so much!"

I can't speak. I choke on my own tears. What in the world was I thinking fighting this thing between me and Danny? How could I not realize how important it is—to both of us?

He finally stops crying and runs his sleeve across his face. I kiss him on the head. "We're both tired, sweetie," I tell him. "Let's go to bed. We'll be able to go visit Danny tomorrow. He'll be out of surgery and ready to see us."

"Okay." He gets up and we both go upstairs.

I take him into his room, but we both stop dead in our tracks when we see four giant, stuffed shopping bags sitting on his bed.

"Um....Mom......?" he stammers.

I peek into the bags. They're full of clothes and shoes in Zeke's size. Everything is in here—pants, shirts, socks, underwear, jackets, hats—everything he needs. I even see a new handheld video game console tucked in there.

I don't have to wonder who bought these even though there's no note or anything like that. Now I know why Ellen left us at the hospital while everyone else stuck around until we heard that Danny was out of surgery.

Neither Zeke nor I touch the bags. "What should we do with it all?" he husks.

I wake up and touch his hair. "Get your pajamas on, sweetie. I'll put this stuff away."

He does it and then goes into the bathroom to brush his teeth.

I go through the bags, but every single item makes me marvel even more that someone cares enough to do this for us. I want to pay Ellen back for this, but I know she wouldn't want that.

She wants to help me and Zeke just like everyone else in the firehouse family.

We're a part of that now. Zeke and I are part of Danny's life and everybody knows it. I don't need to feel ashamed of that and I'm not.

I'm incredibly proud of it. I'll spend every day working to deserve the honor of being part of his life—of being part of all their lives. I just hope I can live up to that.

I finish emptying the last bag when Zeke comes back and climbs into bed. I help tuck him in and he heaves a huge sigh when I sit down on the bed next to him.

He looks out the window and actually smiles. "It's gonna be great when Danny comes home from the hospital."

"Yeah," I murmur. "It will be nice when we're all here together and we don't have to worry about your dad coming after us again."

He breathes out one more time, "Yeah," but he's gazing too blissfully out the window to look at me.

I don't have to wonder what he's thinking about. I'll be thinking the same thing when I go to bed and shut my eyes to go to sleep. I'll be thinking about what it will be like when Danny comes home and the three of us start living here as a family.

I kiss Zeke on the cheek and whisper, "Good night, sweetheart," before I leave the room.

Putting him to bed usually takes longer than this, but I don't want to disturb that beautiful dream. I want him to stay in that fantasy world for as long as possible—forever if he can.

I tiptoe down the hall, glance into the guest room where I've been staying before, and then go into Danny's bedroom.

I find a matching four loaded shopping bags sitting on the bed. They contain clothes for me—jeans, shirts, bras, underwear, shoes, handbags, and even a new phone still in the box. Ellen must have spent a fortune on this.

I can't deal with this right now, so I set all the bags on the floor by the dresser and sit down on the end of the bed. Danny isn't here, but this is our room now. Where else would I sleep, now that we're together and we're going to start building a future together?

This is our room now. I spent last night with him in this room—our first night together as a real couple. He'll come home from the hospital and then we'll share this room every night.

There will be plenty of nights when I'll be here by myself. There will be nights when he's on shift at the firehouse and I'm sleeping here alone thinking and praying that he's safe.

I need to be prepared for that. I need to accept that Danny isn't just my hero. He's everyone's hero. He spends his days and nights out there helping the people who need him. That's what makes him great. I wouldn't love him like this if he was any different.

I could never deprive him of the job he loves. He wouldn't accept that anyway. He wouldn't get together with me if I didn't accept it, so I better grow a spine and deal with it.

I sigh, but I can't bring myself to move. I stare at the bags of clothes sitting on the floor. They confirm everything I've been thinking since yesterday.

I'm a part of this family now. How did I ever get this lucky?

These people will stop at nothing to give us everything we need. If we need anything or if anything bad happens to us, it won't be from a lack of these people trying to make our lives as great as they can be.

I don't want to be anywhere else. I want to be right here in the middle of it and give my all to make that happen for them, too.

I can't keep sitting here all night staring at shopping bags. I finally take off my clothes and lay them in a pile by the door. I've been wearing the same clothes for nearly three weeks. It's time I retired them or at least set them aside for a month or two before I wear them again.

I crawl into bed, switch off the bedside lamp, and curl up under the covers. Danny isn't here, but the bed smells and feels like him. His presence wraps around me exactly the way he would wrap around me if he was here right now.

I shut my eyes. He's with me. He's right here in this bed with his arms around me and his lips on my neck. I feel his skin and hear him breathing. His heat radiates to me from the bed next to me.

We'll always be together even when we're apart. Nothing can stop that now.

Chapter 24: Danny

I crack my eyelids open and instantly regret it when stark, fluorescent hospital lights pierce my brain. I groan and clamp my eyes shut, but it's too late. I'm in the hospital and lying flat on my back. I have no choice but to lie here with those lights glaring down into my eyes.

A shadow passes in front of my face and my eyes open automatically. I pry my eyelids apart just enough to see Ellen leaning over me. "I need you to open your eyes, sweetheart," she tells me. "I need to check your pupils and then you can close your eyes again."

"You do it," I croak. "I can't open them."

She chuckles, forces my eyelids open, and shines her flashlight into my eyes one after the other. "That's it. You're done. You can go back to playing video games now."

I snort. "Don't joke at a time like this. Can't you see I'm injured?"

She laughs. "I can see that your sense of humor is back, so I know you're gonna be okay."

"How about you turn off the lights—or give me a blindfold? Anything!"

She touches my shoulder—the non-injured one. Now that I'm awake, I can feel the bandage taped to my shoulder.

I also feel a million incisions cutting through the muscle where the doctors operated on the gunshot wound.

"You might want to open your eyes," she tells me. "There are a few people here who want to see you."

I don't want to know who's here to see me, but I crack my eyes open a little more and see John and Keith standing next to my bed. "Hey, champ," John murmurs. "How is it?"

"You really don't want to know," I growl. "Is this what I woke up for—you two?"

John steps aside...and I see Zeke and Emily standing behind them. John, Keith, and Ellen stand there smiling at all of us for a minute. Then the three of them leave.

Zeke and Emily step a little closer to the bed. Emily stands behind Zeke with her hands resting on his shoulders.

He stares at me lying there with my shoulder covered in gauze. "Hi, Danny," he croaks.

"Hey, buddy!" I hold out my hand and he crosses the last few feet to the side of my bed. I touch his hair and run my hand down his cheek. I can't stop looking at him. He is definitely worth waking up for. They both are.

"You're all right!" I rasp. "I was so worried that you got hurt."

"We're okay," he tells me. "Thanks to you."

"Cut it out! I'm so relieved you're all right." I look up at Emily. "I got there as soon as I could. I came out of the firehouse garage and glanced down the street. I saw the car pull up in front of the house and I knew it was him. I never should have left you alone....."

She shakes her head fast and tears spring to her eyes. "Don't apologize, whatever you do. You saved our lives."

I move my hand over to her, but she's too far away. I pull her to the bed and then she's bending over me kissing me right in front of Zeke. She must have told him...so everything is all right.

She falls on top of me and sobs into my neck for a few minutes. I rub the back of her neck and run my fingers through her hair. "Shh!" I tell her. "Shhh-sshh! It's all right! You two are all right and I'm all right. Everything's okay. There's nothing to cry about."

She sits up, wipes her face, and nods fast.

"Hey, good news!" I tell her. "You aren't married anymore. Problem solved!"

She bursts out laughing even though she's still crying. "Yeah."

I can't stop touching her face. She's so beautiful and now she's all mine. Both of them are.

I look over at Zeke. He stares back at me. He doesn't act like me kissing his mom is anything unusual. He knows, so we're all good.

I clear my throat, gulp, and look around. "Could you maybe find me a glass of water or something?"

"I'll do it!" Zeke pounces on the side table, pours a glass of water from the pitcher, and puts a straw in it. He holds it for me while I sip the water through the straw.

Ellen comes back while we're in the middle of that. "You can sit up when you're ready, sweetheart. You don't have to lie there like a slug."

"How about you take a flying leap?" I tell her and make her laugh.

She comes over to the bed and pushes a button on the remote control. The head of the bed starts to tip up. "The doctors are going to release you after twenty-four hours of observation, so you might as well get used to being vertical and operational."

"That word isn't in my vocabulary," I grumble.

"It is now. You're going home to recover. You can moan and groan and complain all you want once you get there—but if you give Emily a hard time, I'll hear about it and you won't like the outcome."

Emily glances at her and Ellen shoots her a smirk on the side. "Wonderful," I snarl. "So you and Emily and Leila will all be plotting against me behind my back. Is that how it's going to work from now on?"

"You got it." Ellen kisses me on the top of the head and leaves again. "I'll be back in a few hours to check on you."

She leaves the bed in a semi-reclining, sitting-up position. I finally have no choice but to face the world. I groan again when I pick up my head and look around. No one is here but me, Zeke, and Emily.

They hover around me and Emily sits on the mattress next to me. "Does your shoulder hurt real bad?"

"Not too bad," I grumble. "I mean, yes, it hurts like hell, but they've loaded me up with so many drugs that it isn't too bad."

"How is it going to be when you get home?"

I snort. "I'll piss and moan a lot. That's how it's going to be when I get home." I tip my head back against the pillow and shut my eyes. "Sorry. I shouldn't complain so much. I'm so glad you two are all right. I thought Colin might have done something to you."

"We cleaned the house, Danny," Zeke interjects. "We even put fresh carpet in the living room to cover up .....well, everything."

I have to look up, and when I see him, I wind up smiling. "You did? That's outstanding. Thank you so much. I wasn't looking forward to getting home and seeing a chalk outline in the living room every time I want to put my feet up and watch a movie."

"It isn't chalk," Emily mumbles. "They used spray paint."

"On the carpet?!" I gasp. "Those bastards!" I glance over at Zeke. "Sorry. Don't repeat that."

He bursts into a grin. "You said a lot more bad words at the school."

I find myself blushing and grinning back at him. "You're right. I did. I was really mad at those guys."

"Yeah. I saw."

I laugh. "Hey, they deserved it. Jesus! Spray paint? Who does that?"

"Anyway, you'd have to replace the carpet anyway because of all the stains," Emily goes on.

"But we covered it up," Zeke finishes. "We put down that extra piece of carpet you had in the garage. We just need to get a new frame for your Medal of Valor."

I grin again. "It sounds like you two have my life all organized for me."

He bursts into a matching grin back at me. "Yeah. So you can moan and groan and complain about your shoulder and not worry about anything."

I laugh. "Thanks. It's really nice having you two looking out for me."

"It's really nice having you looking out for us, too." Emily kisses me on the cheek and squeezes my hand. Damn, this is nice! I gotta get myself injured more often.

We hang out in the hospital room and she tells me about all the clothes Ellen bought for both of them. "I better pay her back," I remark.

"Don't," Emily tells me. "I don't think she wants you to."

"I'm sure she doesn't. That's why I have to pay her back."

She squeezes my hand again. "Don't. She's trying to be nice. She doesn't want any money."

I let it drop. Emily is right. Ellen would be hurt if I tried to pay her back.

She comes back later. "The doctors are drawing up your release paperwork now." She hands Emily my car keys. "Here are the keys to Danny's truck. It's parked behind the firehouse where he left it yesterday. You can go get it and some clothes for him to ride home in. As soon as he's released, you can take him home."

Emily turns to me, kisses me right in front of Ellen, and squeezes my hand. "I'll be right back." She gets ready to leave and turns to Zeke. "How about you stay here with Danny until I come back with the truck?"

Zeke grins even more broadly. "Okay! I'll make sure he's all right."

She beams at him. "I'm sure you will." Then she kisses him on the head and leaves us alone.

Chapter 25: Emily

I get a rush of happiness on my way out of the hospital. Zeke will be just fine with Danny even if Danny is injured. Those two were made for each other. Besides, Ellen is there in case anything happens. There are enough people around who will take care of Zeke.

I'm not alone anymore. I don't have to do this all by myself and now Colin is dead. I don't have to guard myself against him anymore.

I ride the elevator to the hospital lobby where I meet John and Keith entering to visit Danny. When they hear what I'm doing, Keith offers to drive me to the firehouse to pick up Danny's truck.

I thank Keith profusely, but he keeps insisting the whole time that it's nothing. "We're family, remember?"

He drops me off and I drive the truck to Danny's house—our house. I pick up a pair of Danny's pajama pants, a pair of tennis shoes and socks, and a giant grey hoodie that will fit over his bandaged shoulder. I don't know if he'll be able to wear the hoodie, but I want him to have it just in case.

I put everything in a bag and head back to the hospital. I walk into the room to find Zeke there alone. Danny's bed is empty. My stomach drops into my shoes. "What happened?!" I gasp. "Where's Danny? Did something happen?"

"He's in the bathroom," Zeke tells me, and right then, I hear the toilet flush in the next room. The water runs into the sink for a second and Danny comes out wearing a pair of hospital pajama pants.

His huge bandage surrounds his shoulder and most of his chest. He isn't wearing anything else above the waist and he has his arm in a sling.

He hobbles over to the bed, sits down, and groans. "Thank you, baby," he tells me when I take his clothes out of the bag.

He takes his pajama pants back into the bathroom and comes out a second later wearing them. He lays the hospital pair across the bed. He can use his other arm just fine.

"Do you want me to help you put your shoes on?" I ask him.

"That would be wonderful." He sits down on the bed.

I take out his socks and shoes. I have to kneel on the floor to tug them over his feet.

I happen to glance up and see his eyes drilling into me. This is such a suggestive position, but neither of us can say anything or act on it right now. We're in a public place with Zeke standing right there.

My cheeks flush when I see the way Danny is looking at me. We're going home together. He might be injured now, but he won't stay that way for long.

We both know what will happen once he recovers. It will probably happen even before then. It will probably happen right away. I don't imagine Danny delaying something like that just because he got shot in the shoulder.

I break eye contact first and get busy tying his shoes. Then he pulls out the hoodie.

"I wasn't sure if you wanted to use it with your arm like that," I tell him.

"It's perfect." He doesn't move his injured arm when he pulls the hoodie on. He keeps his arm and the sling under the hoodie and puts his head and his good arm through the other two holes.

He pulls the hoodie down over his chest and wears it normally except that his injured arm is on the inside. Now he's ready to leave.

Ellen comes back with one of the doctors. "You look downright normal like this," she tells him.

"Very funny," he growls. "I am normal."

She laughs and hands him a clipboard. "You can sign it lefthanded." She turns to me while he signs the paperwork. "Do you have everything you need?"

"Yes. Thank you so much. I don't know how to thank you."

"Just take care of yourselves." She gives me a quick hug and then hands me a slip of paper. "Here's my number, John's, and Keith's. One of us will stop by later and drop off Danny's duffel bag from his locker at the firehouse.....and here is the bag with all his personal effects—everything he had on him when the ambulance brought him in. His phone and everything is in there."

"Thank you," he husks.

She kisses him on the cheek. "You can go home now. One or the other of us will stop by and check on you every now and then. Call us if you need us."

He heaves to his feet and walks slowly out of the hospital. He has to hold onto the elevator rail on our way down to the lobby.

This is probably the only time I'll be able to get away with opening the truck's passenger door for him. He doesn't argue. He just stands there and waits for Zeke to climb into the back and then Danny collapses into the passenger seat.

I drive him home and follow him upstairs with his bags. Zeke goes with us and watches Danny sit down on the bed and then groan when he eases back on the pillows. He shuts his eyes. "Hey, buddy. I would really like to hear some more of *Treasure Island* right now."

"Okay! I'll get it!" Zeke tears away downstairs.

I take this opportunity to lean over Danny. "Are you gonna be okay like this?"

"Yeah, I'll be fine. I just need to rest." His eyes open. "I might need some of your special pain relievers later after Zeke goes to bed."

He glides one hand toward me and squeezes my breast through my shirt. I yelp and pull away. "Watch it, pal. You're supposed to be injured."

He smirks at me. "All the more reason I need a sexy nurse to take extra good care of me."

He grins as I back away. "I have a feeling you're going to be a terrible patient."

"Nonsense. All I have to do is lie here while you give me my treatment."

His eyes dip to my body, but just then, Zeke comes running back with the book. He climbs onto the bed, turns to the right page, and starts reading.

Danny keeps grinning at me behind Zeke's back until I inch out of the room and make a run for it. So I was right. Danny's shoulder won't slow him down at all—not that way.

I go downstairs and go through the kitchen. This is the first time I've had a chance to really check out this house since I'm officially living here now.

I don't have to worry about Colin coming back. Danny is down for the count, so it will be up to me to manage the house until he gets back on his feet.

I go through the fridge and write out a shopping list. I can drive Danny's truck to the grocery store. Zeke can stay with Danny, but I need to talk to Danny about what he likes to eat. We haven't even had that most basic conversation.

I'm just about to make him something for lunch when Zeke comes downstairs with the book. "What's happening upstairs?" I ask. "Did you get sick of reading?"

"Danny wants to sleep. He doesn't feel strong. He's tired and he went to sleep."

"Oh." I blink at my son. "Okay." I guess I can't argue with that.

"Mom?" he asks.

"Yeah?"

He squirms a lot before he finally blurts out. "Today's Monday."

"Yeah? What about it?"

"So....tomorrow's Tuesday."

"Yeah?"

He holds his breath and chokes out, "Could I go to school tomorrow....now that we don't have to worry about Dad anymore?"

I stare at him for a second. Colin isn't coming back. He isn't out there stalking us and trying to kill us.

I have no more reason to protect Zeke—not like that. I'm going to have to get used to a new way of doing things. My brain doesn't want to accept that Colin really is gone.

"Um.....okay, sweetie. I guess you can go to school tomorrow."

"Yes!" Zeke jumps in the air, pumps his fist high, and takes off running to go play outside.

He leaves the house quiet—too quiet—but that's okay because Danny is here. He's right upstairs.

I tiptoe up there and stand out in the hall without entering the bedroom. Danny lies on the bed, sound asleep. He looks fragile and beautiful like this. I want to put my arms around him, but he needs sleep more. He's going to take a long time to recover from getting shot in the shoulder.

He took a bullet to protect me. He threw himself in front of a gun to save my life. I'll never forget that and I love him for it. Letting him sleep is the least I can do for him.

I want to stand here watching him sleep for the rest of both our lives. I never want him out of my sight again—ever—but that isn't going to happen. He belongs to too many other people.

He belongs to Zeke, the firehouse, the people he rescues, and the rest of the world. I don't get to keep Danny all to myself. He has too much to give.

I tiptoe back downstairs and go back to organizing the house. I have a few other things to do to get Zeke ready to go to school tomorrow.

This is how my life is going to be from now on—organizing Zeke's lunch for tomorrow and Danny's gear for work and every other detail of our daily existence. It all seems so normal.

I'm going to take a while to get used to having a normal life, too. I don't have to run and hide from Colin anymore. I'll just stay here with Danny and live normal life. I can live with that.

Epilogue: Emily

I hold Danny's hand—his good hand. His other arm hangs in the sling, but he's wearing regular clothes today with his arm outside his Fire Department T-shirt.

Zeke strides ahead of us with his new school lunchbox inside the new school backpack Ellen bought for him. We don't know what else he needs, but I guess we're about to find out.

He walks as fast as he can in front of us heading for the school gate. He can't wait to get there.

The school is right down the block from our house, so I don't picture Danny and me walking Zeke to school much in the future. Today is a special day, though, so we're both walking with him.

He gets as far as the front gate and stops. He eyes all the kids playing on the playground, but he doesn't go in there.

Danny steps forward, takes his hand out of mine, and lays it on Zeke's shoulder. "You okay, buddy?"

Zeke nods and glances up at Danny. "It's weird. I still think Dad is out there somewhere even when he isn't."

"That's normal," Danny tells him. "It will be like that for a long time. Ask your mom. She's going through the same thing. Hey, even I have to remind myself that he isn't out there. I keep thinking I need to do something to stop him from coming back for us."

"Really?" Zeke asks. "It happens to you, too?"

"Yeah." Danny squats down in front of him and runs his hand down Zeke's arm. "Everything is gonna work out. You'll see."

"I know," Zeke mumbles. "I don't know why it bothers me."

"It bothers you because your life is changing. You lived a certain life for a long time and now it's ending so a new life can start. That takes time. It bothers you because you're used to the old life and you aren't used to the new life yet, but you will get used to it. Pretty soon, it will seem normal to you and it won't bother you anymore. Okay?"

Zeke nods down at the ground and then looks up. "Thanks, Danny."

"You bet, pal." He hugs Zeke. "You're gonna have a great day today and you already know these kids and they know you. They know what's going on with you and they're all there to help you. Kids from the firehouse are here, so if you have a problem, you can talk to them. Right?"

Zeke nods again.

"Hey, look." Danny turns around and points down the street in both directions. "Our house is right over there and the firehouse is right over there. You can see them both from the playground. If anything happens, you can go to either of those places and find someone to help you. You know that. Whatever happens, you're gonna be okay."

"Yeah," Zeke husks. "I know."

"Okay, good." Danny hugs him one more time. "Have a great day, buddy. I'm proud of you. I'll see you when you get out this afternoon."

Zeke hugs him back. "Bye, Danny." Then Zeke hugs me. "Bye, Mom."

"Bye, sweetie," I tell him. "Have a great day. I'll see you this afternoon."

He takes off and I slip my hand back into Danny's. We both stand at the gate watching Zeke walk onto the school grounds. He disappears into the classroom and comes out without his backpack.

He takes off running onto the playground, and in a second, he gets all mixed up with all the kids from the firehouse that he met at the beach.

"He probably won't like it if we stand here watching him," Danny remarks. "We should disappear."

"Yeah, we should," I reply. "How are you feeling? Are you sure you feel good enough to walk around out here in broad daylight? Shouldn't you go back to your vampire coffin for another hundred years?"

He snorts with laughter and turns to grin at me. "Don't start shooting off at the mouth. I get enough of that from the fire crew."

I grin back at him and wind up blushing. "You were the one who said you wanted me to be a part of this. What did you think was going to happen?"

He pretends to roll his eyes and groan. "Sweet Jesus! What have I gotten myself into?"

I laugh and kiss him. "Seriously. Don't exhaust yourself. You're supposed to be recovering."

"I won't exhaust myself. My shoulder is injured, not the rest of me. I can still walk...and do a few other things....." He slips his arm around my waist and pulls me against his body.

"Not here!" I squeal. "We're standing in front of the dang school, for God's sake!"

He laughs, kisses me, and lets me go. "Fine. You can act all virtuous out here in public, but I know the truth."

Now I really do blush. I can't stop myself from slipping both arms around his waist. "Come on. You know you want to keep that a secret all to yourself. You wouldn't like it if anyone found out what I was really like."

His cheeks color and he bites his lip to hold back another wicked grin. "You're right. That is all mine."

We start kissing again, but when it starts to heat up, we both pull away. "The sound of children yelling and laughing in the background kinda kills the mood, doesn't it?" he remarks.

I slip my hand back into his. "Let's go home. No one will see us there and you can be as bad a patient as you want."

"Will you dress up as a nurse for me?"

I laugh at him. "I'll have to make the costume first."

I expect him to laugh and turn it into another sexual innuendo, but instead, he stops in his tracks and uses my hand to pull me around to face him. "Baby.....I'm going down to the firehouse for a while."

"What?! Why? You aren't working today. Don't tell me you think you're gonna work with your shoulder cut to pieces."

"I'm not going there to work. I'm going there to check in with John and Keith and the rest of the crew."

I frown at him, but before I can protest, he slips his fingers into my hair and kisses me again.

That kiss silences my protests. Of course he wants to go to the firehouse. He's a red-blooded man who loves his work. He can't work because he's injured, but he won't be happy if he doesn't at least see his friends and family and check in with them.

He eases back and his lips trail off my mouth. He takes another split second before he opens his eyes.

Those eyes drill me to the core. I can't deny him anything when he looks at me like that. "Go home," he murmurs. "I'll be back in a little while. Don't worry about me. I'll be fine."

"Okay," I breathe. "I love you."

"I love you, too." He kisses me one more time. "I'll see you when I get home."

He walks away with his usual direct, purposeful gait. He looks exactly the same as he always does except that he for the sling over his arm.

He won't stay down for long. Ellen is right about that. Nothing can keep Danny down.

I watch him walk a block away and then I turn in the other direction. He doesn't want me pining over him. He wants to know that I'm okay and happy at home while he's at work.

I go back to the house and start cleaning it up. I start in our bedroom and work my way down. I'm just thinking about going outside and doing some yard work when someone knocks on the front door.

I peek through the blinds and see Ellen standing on the porch. She bursts into a huge smile when I answer the door. "Hey!" she greets me. "I just saw Danny walking into the firehouse and Zeke at school. Do you have any plans for today?"

"No, but you already went shopping for us. We don't need anything else."

"I'm not here to shop. Do you mind if I come in?"

"Uh....sure." I stand back to make room for her.

She limps into the house. "What are you up to today?" she asks again.

"Um...nothing. I just cleaned the house and I was about to go outside and do some yard work. No one has done anything since the fire." I frown at her. "Is there a reason you came over here?"

She shoots me another grin, crosses to Danny's bookshelf, takes a book off the shelf, and lets it fall onto the coffee table. It's a giant slab of a book and it falls with a heavy thump that rattles the coffee table.

"This," Ellen tells me. "This is the reason I came over here."

I stare down at the book. The title reads, *Emergency Care of the Sick and Injured.* There's a picture on the cover of three emergency workers treating someone who is strapped to a backboard. A giant collar surrounds the person's neck and blood stains the patient's face.

"What is this?" I ask.

"This is Danny's copy of the EMT certification textbook. He told me you wanted to start doing your EMS training." She sits down on the couch and unlocks her knee joint to bend her leg. "That's why I'm here."

"No, no. I couldn't."

She gives me a hard look and dips her chin to the couch next to her. "Sit down, Emily."

She says it in such a commanding tone that I can't argue. I sink onto the couch next to her and she swivels around to face me.

"Listen to me," she tells me. "You've been living someone else's life for years. You've been a prisoner in your own home. You've been living in fear for your life and the life of your son. You haven't had a chance to pursue a career or your dreams. Now's your chance."

"You don't understand," I tell her. "I can't do this. I didn't even graduate from high school."

"If you don't do this, you'll destroy every good thing you have with Danny right now. You're grateful to him for taking you in and saving you and Zeke from Colin, but that won't last. That isn't the basis for you to have an ongoing relationship with him. You won't be happy staying home, cleaning the house, and doing yard work. You need something for yourself. You need a passion and a dream of your own that you can pursue. You won't be happy with Danny or anyone else if you don't have that. You'll feel trapped and you'll come to resent Danny. You'll think he's keeping you a prisoner just as much as Colin did." She pulls the book toward me and opens it in front of me. "This is what you're really interested in. Zeke will grow up and become more independent. When that happens, you'll need something of your own—something that gets you fired up—something that gives your life some purpose and direction."

She flips the pages and I find myself staring down at all the colorful diagrams, photographs, and drawings.

She turns to the first chapter. "This page lists the career pathway from Basic First Aid to Paramedic. You can see that, between First Aid and EMT, it lists First Responder, but you don't have to worry about that. The EMT certification course covers the First Responder training, too, so it's included."

I stare down at the page. The flow chart goes down the list of all the different grades and classifications of paramedics in all the different branches of the emergency service.

The hospital paramedic branch leads to Physician Assistant and eventually Doctor. The field service branch leads to Rescue Helicopter Paramedic, Advanced Rescue Flight Paramedic, Critical Care Paramedic, and eventually leads to Doctor.

Could I really do something like that?

Everything I knew about my life changes in a split second. Ellen is right. Danny must have realized it, too, if he told her what I said about wanting to become a paramedic.

He must have known all along that I wouldn't be happy staying home. He did know. He told me that first night when he brought me here from the shelter.

He said no one who dreams about working in the emergency services would ever be happy doing anything else. He said once they start, they don't go back.

He must know I won't be happy, not even with him, if I don't pursue my own dream.

Before I can even take my eyes off the page, Ellen pulls a folder from her bag. "This is the enrollment form for the certification program. John is holding a community First Aid course at the firehouse at the end of the month. The course is free and open to the public. All you have to do is tell him and he'll put your name on the list. The First Aid course is the only prerequisite for the certification program."

She puts the folder in front of me on top of the book. Then she pats my arm. "You can study up on this book in the meantime. You can call me or Leila if you have any questions about any of it."

She gives my wrist a little squeeze and walks out of the house. Her leg brace makes a clunking noise on the porch and I hear her walk down to the driveway. She starts her car and drives away.

Now I'm sitting here staring at these papers in front of me. The enrollment form for the EMT certification program looks straightforward enough. It doesn't even ask what education level I have.

I flip through the enrollment form and then lay it aside to look at the book. My heart starts racing as I turn to the first page. It goes through the different branches of the emergency services sector, including Fire, Police, Hospital, and Search and Rescue services.

I get more and more interested the further I read. Then I get to the medical section of the book.

Before I know it, I'm up to my eyelids in biology, chemistry, physics, and a whole lot of other stuff. This is way beyond anything I learned in school, but it's so fascinating that I can't stop reading.

I'm still reading when Zeke bursts into the house. He throws his backpack on the floor. "I'm going to Felix's house, Mom! His mom said she would call Danny to tell him where I was. See you later!"

He charges straight out the door without asking my permission. I call, "Wait a second....!" but he's already gone.

He leaves the front door standing open, and when I get there, I see him running down the street to catch up with another boy. They go off together.

I recognize the boy from the beach. He's Cameron and Olivia Santiago's son.

That settles it. I really need to step up and be a normal part of this community.

I go upstairs and get the phone Ellen bought for me. I bring the box down to the living room, take out the phone, and go through a long process of setting it up.

Then I find the piece of paper Ellen gave me at the hospital—the one with her, John's, and Keith's phone numbers on it. I enter the numbers into the phone and send each of them a text telling them that this is my new number.

Ellen texts back immediately. She sends me a smiley-faced emoji, then an emoji jumping up and down and cheering, and then she texts me back with Danny's number.

I send her another text telling her that Zeke is going to Felix's house and could Ellen please give me Cameron's and Olivia's numbers, too.

Ellen texts me, *I have a better idea,* and sends me a PDF attachment.

It's the contact sheet for the whole firehouse, including the phone numbers of all the Fire Department personnel, parents, spouses, and administrative people.

I stare at it for a second. This is real. I'm going to have all these people's names and phone numbers in my phone from now on.

Danny doesn't have any extra numbers next to his name, but my name and number will appear on this sheet pretty soon.

Thinking that makes me so happy. I trust these people with my life. I don't have to worry about any of them having my number because

Colin isn't out there looking for me or trying to call me up to threaten my life.

I send Ellen a, *Thanks,* text and then I text Olivia. She's super nice about Zeke coming over and sends me her address. She also asks if I want her to send Zeke home at a certain time. This is all so normal and I guess that's what I am now. I'm normal.

Danny comes back a little while later, takes one look at me reading the EMT certification textbook, and goes upstairs without saying anything.

I go back to reading. It will be like this from now on. I have a future to look forward to and I can't wait.

<u>End of Book 3.</u>

If you enjoyed this book, please consider leaving a review. You can also support me on Patreon at <u>www.patreon.com/InvisiblePublishing</u>.

Keep Reading

Firehouse Blues Series: Book 4: Starting Over

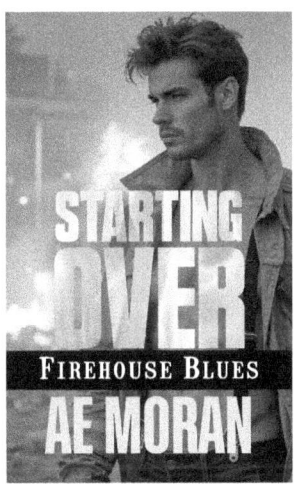

When a mysterious stranger comes out of nowhere to save the day at the last second....

Paramedic Chris Daniels has all she needs—or so she thinks. No one is happy about a stranger coming into the firehouse community and shaking things up—until they meet fellow paramedic Josh Abbott. The firehouse will never be the same when the crew discovers that Josh isn't what he seems—even if he's one of the most competent firefighter paramedics they've ever had the privilege of working with.

When their worlds collide, the cocktail of their hidden pasts could become the bomb that blows the firehouse apart—which could turn out to be the best thing that's ever happened to them. Chris and Josh must confront the ghosts of the past, but the ghosts don't want to be laid to rest. They'll keep coming back and try to steal any happiness Chris and Josh might find with each other. Chris and Josh will have to fight with all they have to preserve what they value most.

You can find it at your favorite book retailer.

Get All of AE Moran's Free Books

S ign Up Once—Get all A.E. Moran's free books including brand new releases

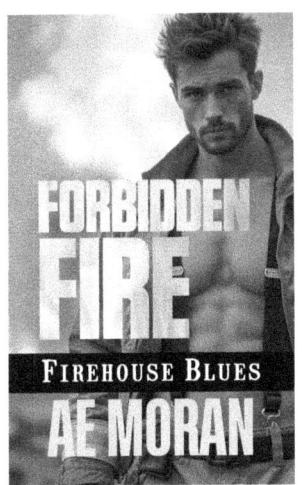

When what you want most is the one thing you can never have......

Austin McAuliffe is every woman's dream firefighter—young, strong, drop-dead hot, and selflessly dedicated to his career—and to the woman of his heart, Emma Brady. Only one other person holds a place in Austin's life—his best friend and fellow firefighter, Theo Gough. Austin insists on Theo spending time with Austin and Emma as a couple, especially when these two firefighters have a hard day at the office.

No one can believe when Austin completely flips out and randomly accuses Theo and Emma of flirting with each other in front of the whole fire crew. Could there be some deeper, more sinister reason for Austin to suddenly lose his mind and lash out at those closest to him?

Emma is devastated when Austin coldly dumps her with no warning and disappears out of her life, but Austin casts a long shadow. The nightmare of his sudden betrayal will come back to haunt Emma and Theo long after Austin is gone. Will the ghosts of the past ruin any chance for them to regain their happiness.....or will Austin's madness take down everyone he cares about along with him?

Sign up at www.authoraemoran.com to read it for free.

About AE Moran

A.E Moran is the contemporary romance pen name for Theo Mann.

I write 70 books per year—and yes, before you ask, all these books are my original creative work. Nothing written under my name is AI-generated or ghostwritten because I write better than AI and any ghostwriter out there.

People don't read fiction for entertainment or to escape from reality. People read fiction to see their humanity reflected in another person's character and story.

This is my promise to you. When you read my books, you'll see your own humanity reflected in the characters and stories. I take this commitment to my readers very seriously. My books are an intimate form of communication between us. I would never disrespect my readers by turning that over to a machine or another writer. This is my bond between me and you as my reader.

I write 20,000 words per day as my daily work output. If anyone with a public platform would like to challenge me to prove this in a controlled environment, feel free to contact me on this website's contact page.

I worked as a professional ghostwriter for fifteen years. Now I'm going for the Guinness World Record by writing 700 books over the next ten years and 1400 books over the next twenty years, all originally written by me. See my website for the full book list.

I'm also the author of *Proof for the Existence of God* and the *Crimes Against Fiction* blog. You can find all my nonfiction work at www.crimes-against-fiction.com.

If you have a story idea, or if you would like me to explore a series in more depth, or if you'd like me to explore a character by writing a spinoff series about that character or world, leave me a message on my website's contact page. I answer all reader emails, so ask me anything, tell me what you liked and didn't like, and let me know where you'd like your favorite series to go. I would love to hear your ideas and find out what you'd like to read next.

You can find out more at www.theomann.com or at www.authoraemoran.com.

Also by AE Moran (so far)